CONTENTS

SEDUCING THE CECAELIA HEIR

May Matthews

CHAPTER ONE

TABITHA

Glow worms coat the walls and ceiling of the ballroom-sized cavern like a second skin, illuminating the expectant faces of the audience in a soft purple glow. Thousands are in attendance — the whole pod of cecaelia have come to hear Mother's proclamation. They shift on their tentacles and murmur in hushed tones as they wait for her to begin. It takes physical effort to remain stoic like the princess I am. The anticipation has me itching to fidget with a tentacle or play with my hair.

But I don't. Everyone needs to see me as a capable leader, like Mother, who is a fair and efficient queen, and has the support of all her people.

The thing is, she's getting older, and pieces are shifting now. Cecaelia monarchs may only serve until the age of fifty. A rule that ensures our society is always moving forward, never dwelling in the past. Everyone wants to be the first to hear what this new era holds in store for them, which is why they're all here tonight. It's why I'm here with my twin. This is what we've been waiting our whole lives for.

Mother stands tall on her muscular plum-coloured tentacles as she addresses the crowd. She truly embodies power and confidence with her broad shoulders and charcoal black hair falling in waves down her bare chest. Humans have fictionalized the cecaelia race over the years to be nothing more than evil singing octo-people, but that's not right. Yes, there's the whole upper body of a human and lower half of an octopus thing, but we're not inherently evil and we're not fictional. We're just a race of ten-limbed creatures trying to live in peace and be happy.

My sister Cecelia is Mother's smaller look-a-like. Everyone is expecting her to be chosen as the next Queen. Cece and I flank Mother on stage, standing when she stands, sitting when she sits, like a school of fish always in sync. But where Cece echoes Mother's fierce confidence, I feel like an imposter trying to convince the world I'm really in the running to be Queen.

"The time has come for my reign as your queen to end." Mother's strong voice echoes off the walls of the cavern, the room suddenly full of her presence. "Upon the eve of my fiftieth birthday, I will pass the crown to one of my daughters to become the next great queen of this pod."

Murmurs burble from the crowd, and Cece and I shoot each other a look of challenge as Mother continues.

Cecelia desperately wants to be the next queen, just like me. It's what we've both been training for all twenty-four years of our lives. Instead of playing tag in the tall seaweed with the other children, Cece and I spent our early childhood learning how to behave like proper princesses in front of our pod. As teenagers, we didn't attend lessons with the other students because we were too busy shadowing Mother, learning the big names of the cecaelia in pods closest to us, and analyzing the policies they'd recently passed. For as long as I can remember, we've wanted nothing more than to be the next queen. It's the only future we've been allowed to dream of and I can't imagine things any other way.

Despite being twins, Cece and I couldn't be more different. Where I've put stock in researching the ecology of our home and have an interest in creating a healthier physical environment, Cece has focused on networking and making political connections with other cecaelia pods. We'll see whose method proves superior when Mother chooses the next queen.

Not that she's yet given any indication as to how she'd go about making that decision. We're both hoping she'll give us some sort of clue today. It's only causing me major stress, sleepless nights, and indigestion. No biggie.

Under normal circumstances, cecaelia pods function within a matriarchal succession in which the first-born daughter becomes heir. My family is different however, because Cecelia and I are twins and we hatched from the same one egg. Cece emerged from our egg big and healthy, while my tiny body barely made it through those first few days. Despite our differences, we both hold claim to the throne. It's up to Mother to choose which of us will become queen after her retirement.

"—which is why," Mother continues, "your new queen will be whichever of my two daughters can impress me the most at my birthday eve soiree in one month's time. I look forward to seeing everyone there. Good evening."

I look to Cecelia who shrugs, just as confused as me. This wasn't right. She was supposed to just choose between us. And what does she mean by *impress her*?

Panic seizes control of my body as I rush after Mother, whose tentacles have carried her all the way to the cavern's waterway exit behind the raised stage. She already has a cecaelia man on her arm. He holds up his front tentacles to carry her waterproof pack — something she and many other cecaelia have at all times to keep their phones and other hydrophilic items safe — which gives everyone a perfect view of his dick, hard and on display. Our race really has no shame in the simple pleasures.

"Mother, wait," I shout after her, social decorum forgotten. I need answers.

My behaviour gets her attention as she turns on me in an instant. "Tabitha, mind your manners," she scolds, towering above me like the strict but loving parent she's always been. "And fix your hair, you look like a rambunctious child."

Ok, ouch. I know she wasn't referring to my a-cups, but I resist the urge to cross my arms over by bare chest. I've accepted my body for what it is years ago.

Cecelia appears behind me and snickers.

I roll my eyes, brushing my fingers through my short black bob to tame it. It's not like the audience can see us over here, and I doubt Mother's arm candy cares.

Wait, was he the bartender from the sushi bar?

Oh well, it doesn't matter. Just about everyone's slept with everyone else in the pod.

"Apologies Mother, we simply request clarification on our task to impress you?" It comes out like a question, and I hate how tentative I sound.

"Correction, dear sister. I have no questions. I'm just here to watch you flounder," Cece says.

Mother sighs. "It's like I said: impress me. I don't care how. Dance, invent something, find a new trade partner for our pod, just for the love of Poseidon don't sing. Nobody deserves the torture of enduring that."

Again, *ouch*. My singing isn't *that* bad.

"Now if you'll excuse me, I have urgent business with Lionel here and an appointment with the mage to check over the protection wards soon."

If the tightness of Lionel's balls is any indication, this is urgent indeed.

"I'm expecting great things from the both of you next week," Mother finishes. Then she slinks into the circular pool of water and disappears into the tunnel system that connects the cavern chambers of our community.

Mine and Cecelia's personal guards take up position at our sides as if we can't be trusted to be alone together. They're not exactly wrong. While I love my twin, we both know we'd go to great lengths to ensure our victory. I don't mean homicide or anything, we're not monsters. Just some light sabotage; perhaps a couple slumber shade leaves slipped into the tea or something.

I take my guard, Dominic, by the arm, and together we swim the community tunnels until we arrive at my chambers. Most cecaelia prefer to reside under water or at the very least in the dimly lit caverns where they're safe from cocky orcas and rogue jellyfish, but I prefer something greener. Something fresher.

I emerge first from the water tunnel. Warm sunlight filters into the room, illuminating my forest of plants and rows of haphazardly packed bookshelves. The ceiling of the rocky chamber had caved in years before my birth and that hole in the ceiling is now dripping in lush green vines. This is my happy place.

"So what's the plan, Tabby?" Dom asks, pushing aside the tail end of a pipevine to flop onto my bed of giant bubble coral. The squishy mass of teal orbs jostle under his weight.

Dom and I grew up together as close friends, so when he became my bodyguard, I'd ordered him to drop formalities when we're alone.

Working within a hierarchical monarchy with your friend below you can get weird, so we play at being equals when we can.

Besides, Dom is like my suave and stoic older brother. He isn't bulky like Cecelia's bodyguard, but his slender frame is solid muscle, and he's fast enough to take down any threat before they can lift a tentacle.

"I don't know what to do, Dom." I rub the stress from my face and let out a frustrated moan. "I don't know how I can win this one. Cecelia's been flirting with a prince from that upper coast pod, so I'm sure she'll just get engaged, solidify a new alliance, and call it a day. She wouldn't even break a sweat." I check on my tank of seagrass and run my fingers through the soft green strands. Their simple emotions absorb into my fingertips at my touch: contentedness, serenity, a tiny touch of stress.

While cecaelia all have different gifts, like Cece who can bind others to contracts or Dom who has great strength, I was lucky enough to be born an empath. Feeling the emotions of my plants helps me cultivate a healthy, thriving space. One day I might figure out how to use my gift to my advantage in social situations instead of getting stressed out and overwhelmed all the time.

"I could try rushing my experiments for a sustainable plastic alternative made from seagrass?" I adjust the solar powered UV lamp aimed at the tank. It's far from a solid plan though because who's to say this batch will yield the optimal results I'm looking for? Cecaelia pods all around the world have been suffering from plastic pollution for decades now. Our pod's mage — the cecaelia who uses their gift to put protective camouflaging wards around our caverns to hide them from humans — visited a healer last week to remove microplastics imbedded in his intestinal tract. If only I had more time to get this ready for Mother's soiree. "I don't know, please tell me you have a more realistic idea."

"I'm telling you, you can't go wrong spiking her body wash with yellow dye. She'll look so sickly, that pod prince will be too nervous to go near her," Dom says.

"If we don't think of anything better, that's not the worst back up plan, I guess. But I'd feel a lot better about winning the crown by being more impressive than Cece instead of by sabotaging the competition."

"You and your honorable conscience will be the death of me, girl. We both know Cecelia would do it to you if it would help her game."

"That's a good point," I hold up a finger, "but I'm a bigger person than she is and won't stoop to her level. And now that you've brought it up, you're in charge of testing my soaps and shampoos before I use them. I can't take any chances right now."

"Anything for you, Princess," he deadpans.

I pluck the few strands of black diseased seagrass that have developed and hurl them at Dom who fluidly bats them away with a swipe of a tentacle.

"Okay, okay, let's compromise then. I'll tell you a life-altering secret if you'll let me just put your bathroom products behind lock and key. I don't want to be dyed yellow any more than you do."

There is absolutely nothing about Dom I don't already know.

"Is your secret that one of the suckers on your tentacles tastes things differently than the rest? Because I already know that." I flop onto my bed next to him and give his head a pat.

"It's true, everything tastes saltier with that sucker — but that's not it." He shoots me a cocky grin. "This secret is going to win you the crown, guaranteed."

CHAPTER TWO

BLYTHE

The backyard hasn't been so alive with people in my whole three months of living here. It wasn't the original plan to move into Walton Manor after Grandma died and left it empty. But I also hadn't counted on my boyfriend being a cheating prick. After I found him on the kitchen island with my cook under him at our flat back in Toronto, I hopped on the first plane to Passions Bay and had my people send my things after me. Once upon a time, Chuck's go-getter attitude was the most attractive thing about him. It's how he won me over with elaborately planned dates, and later was how he took his trust fund and nearly doubled it in six years with the right investments. Now, however, that same drive has given him the delusional idea to throw a surprise housewarming party for me on the back lawn of Walton Manor, in hopes of winning me back.

How did he track me down?

No idea.

I'd been radio silent on social media since I got here. This poor bougie beach town has now been tainted by his presence, and I can't help but hate him for it.

"Blythe, it's marvelous to meet you, I'm an old friend of your grandmother's. Live just down the lane in the big grey house," says an elderly woman I've never seen in my life. "I just wanted to say how nice it was to hear a Walton had moved back here. Gosh you look just like she did back in the day, like a young Helen Mirren is what I think, such a beauty."

I fight the urge to roll my eyes. She's laying it on a little thick, but I let her ramble. "Oh and the way that fella of yours tracked down one of your great grandmother's pieces," she whistles.

I follow her admiring gaze to the seven-foot-tall stone statue of a half-octopus lady Chuck obnoxiously had put in the middle of the yard. It really was a beautifully crafted statue that sung of ferocity and power, one created by my great grandma's hand. Bringing it back here would have been a nice gesture, had it not been a desperate bribe to win me back.

I give the woman a tight-lipped smile and carry on wandering through the crowd of wealthy strangers. I would have loved to bail on this event, but it would have felt too much like disrespecting the manor, and more importantly, Grandma's good name. So I bite my tongue and mingle with people who don't actually know me and who only care about being seen at Walton Manor. That is until I accidentally catch Chuck's eye, and he starts toward me.

I can practically feel my blood pressure rising at the thought of having to talk to him right now. I scan my surroundings, then swiftly disappear into the crowd for a quick getaway and make to hide behind the grazing table beside the pool.

In my haste, I hear a sickening snap and suddenly one of my designer heels is a flat and I am falling slow motion into the pool. Fan-fucking-tastic.

I squeeze my eyes shut as the world tips sideways and the smell of chlorine fills my nostrils.

If I had to put a title to my autobiography at this very moment, it would be called *Falling is Never It.* Let's face it, falling into a pool in front of people who have the financial means to make or break you? Not it. Falling in love with Chuck? Also not it. I've been falling ever since he cheated and I walked out on my art gallery, my friends, and my whole life to come here and breathe. And to wallow. It sucks and is not it.

I've been falling for a really long time, I should be submerged by now.

But I never hit the water.

A woman has me by the wrist and yanks me back to a vertical position.

I immediately dive under the table, hidden by the white linen tablecloth, praying to Yahweh or Poseidon or whatever deity is out there that nobody saw that. My pulse is acting like it's at an absolute rager.

A split second later my hero crawls under the table and sits in the grass beside me.

My face flushes hot.

"You're welcome," the five-foot-nothing woman sings. "And yes, I suppose I'll let you share my hiding spot since that was mildly embarrassing." Her black siren eyes twinkle with humour.

My gaze travels over her plump nude lips stretched up in a smirk and I momentarily forget how to form words. I have to force my gaze away from that pretty mouth to take in the rest of this little water goddess. From her short black hair slicked back perfectly to look like she just emerged from the ocean, to the plunging neckline and high slits of her gold dress that clings to her perfectly, showing off her tiny frame — I'm speechless.

"Earth to Ariel, do you speak?" The woman says it in a joking tone, but as soon as the words are out, her eyes widen in horror. "Oh my god, that was so insensitive of me." She starts signing along to her words now. "I apologize, Miss. I did not mean to sound like an ablest twat. I just sometimes say things without much thought and — wait it sounds like I'm trying to make excuses, and I'm not!"

The woman's dainty hands and mouth are flying at a million miles a minute and it's so adorable, a small part of me wants to watch her panicked rambling for hours. But she did just save me from a watery social death so I decide to let her out of her misery.

"I can talk!" I blurt out, "and hear too, for the record. Though when it comes to sight, well, these are contacts." I point to my eyes. "Don't tell anyone."

Her hands freeze in mid-sign and then she slowly lowers them to her lap.

"You really thought you were playing it cool for a second there, didn't you," I tease.

Her entire person relaxes and she looks away "Busted. I suppose I'll have to do better at the next party I crash."

I cock a brow. "Alright, you have my attention..."

She catches the playfulness in my voice and looks me in the eye with a shy smile.

"Tabitha."

"Blythe," I return, and I'm relieved to see no glimmer of recognition at my name. She really is a party crasher then. Interesting.

She lifts my hand to her lips and plants a soft kiss on the back of it, like we're not hiding under a table like a couple of delinquents. "It's a pleasure to meet you, Blythe. Oh, hold still."

Tabitha leans over and brings her face so close to mine that I can smell the mint on her breath. But then she touches the bare skin of my shoulder and a shiver rolls through me. Tabitha notices too, because her face is suddenly just as red as the ladybug she just plucked from my shoulder.

"Oh, there was a bug on me. Fuck, I thought you were about to—" I take a breath, reevaluating what I was just about to admit. "You know what, it doesn't matter. Thank you."

Heat floods my face too. What the actual fuck is happening right now? Since when do I get flustered being introduced to someone I've literally never heard of before? I didn't even flinch when I met Zendaya at that charity event last year.

"Oh, your shoe," she says, looking down to my broken pump. She darts out from beneath the table and returns a second later. "Here. Maybe it can be fixed."

In her hand is the heal of my Louis Vuitton, gleaming red and black.

"That's really not necessary," I start.

Before I know it, she's on her hands and knees, pulling off my broken shoe, and holding the pieces together like some sort of puzzle she can fix.

"This is totally repairable." She holds it up to me. "See the break was so clean, you can glue it back together and nobody would know the difference—"

Glass clinks above our heads as someone helps themselves to the platters of finger foods. Tabitha presses her lips together, remembering that we're supposed to be hiding.

I hold my breath. The sounds fade away as the person leaves, and this gorgeous stranger and I burst out laughing.

"You know, those shoes were uncomfortable anyway. If you want to fix them up and pawn them or something, go for it."

Her perfectly arched brows pull together in confusion. "Why would I do that? If they're uncomfortable, you should just throw them out. There's no sense in selling them to cause someone else the pain of wearing them."

She says it so earnestly, with all the innocence in the world and I have to wonder where this woman came from. Either she's not hurting for money, or she has no idea what she's holding in her hand right now."

"Alright then." I shrug. "Toss them."

"Right now?"

I slip off my other shoe and creep out from beneath the table, checking to make sure the coast is clear. Most of the guests have congregated near the bar and aren't paying any attention to us. Tabitha follows behind.

Bingo.

A few dozen feet away is a wrought iron garbage can. Without hesitating, I pull back my arm and hurl the heel through the air. The shoe hits its mark, landing in the trash can with an audible *thwunk*. Tabitha looks impressed and her enthusiasm doubles as she follows suit, hurling the broken shoe through the air. But this woman is no baseball player. Her aim is way off and the shoe ends up making contact with a glass of champagne in Chuck's hand. The prick doesn't know what hit him when the sparkling drink spills all over his designer polo and white shorts. He keeps his composure pretty well, but years living with the man have me trained to spot the fury simmering just beneath the surface.

Tabitha lets out a gasp at the same time I squeal with delight. I feel like a fucking teenager watching the boy I hate fail gym class, but I don't care. I want to kiss Tabitha for it. Scratch that, I just want to kiss Tabitha.

I wave off whatever she's about to say. "That was the divine intervention of karma, he deserved it." I shoot her a devious grin and am delighted when her smile grows too. It's the kind of smile that makes her look like she's glowing, like everything around her gets brighter too just by being in her vicinity. I immediately know that I need to make her smile like that again. No. I want to taste that smile on her lips.

I'm about to ask if she wants a drink, when I hear Chuck say my name in a microphone and my blood runs cold.

Good lord, he's giving a speech. That was a fucking quick recovery.

Just like that, my fun is over. It's time to say goodbye to Blythe-the-party-crasher-accomplice and be *The Blythe Walton* again.

"Blythe cupcake, where are you?" His tinny voice fills the yard and I want to gag at his use of the pet name.

As much as I want to stay here with Tabitha, I can't ruin a party on my family estate by going AWOL.

I give Tabitha an apologetic look as I stand and straighten my dress that had bunched around my thighs. I'm not sure if I'm projecting, but I swear I see a brief glimmer of attraction as her eyes flick to my full thighs.

I shake it off. There's no time for that right now, one way or another.

I'm about to leave from behind the bar when Tabitha lifts my ankle and slips a kitten heel onto my foot. I watch as she takes off the other one and puts it on my other foot. I'm not sure if I'm more surprised by the act of generosity or by the fact that we're somehow the same shoe size.

"Thank you," I mouth, realizing now I was about to face the entire party barefoot.

"If you need to get out of here later, meet me on the beach by the southern cliff at sunset," she whispers.

At those words, heat blooms between my legs, my pussy begging me to say yes. An escape from Chuck is exactly what I need and the thought of getting away with such a beautiful woman alone in the dark is more than I could have hoped for.

"I'll try," I mouth back before heading off toward the biggest douchebag the world has ever known.

CHAPTER THREE

TABITHA

The lust and gratitude that radiated from Blythe as she walked away sparked my own arousal. I don't know what came over me. I hadn't planned on talking to any humans, let alone asking one to meet me alone after the party. What were we even going to do on the beach? Yes, I slept around just as much as any other cecaelia, which is to say frequently. But not with humans. Nothing could ever come from hooking up with a human. What would I do with only four other limbs anyway? This competition for the crown must have me going crazy.

Once all attention is turned away from the finger foods table, I draw up beside Dom who looks smug, leaning against the pool shed in his tux. He's quite attractive in his human form. Like me, he shifted form to swap his tentacles for legs. The transformation causes us to lose a few inches of height, making me infuriatingly small, but it renders us identical to humans. One look at his face tells me he saw my entire encounter with Blythe.

"I don't need to hear it!" I give him a playful shove.

He holds up his hands in defense. "I wasn't going to say anything!" He looks down at my bare feet. "Just that hooking up with some human woman isn't going to compete with Cecelia marrying a pod prince. If you need some relief, I'm always right here, Princess. All you have to do is ask."

I'd slept with Dom on a number of occasions. He has always been a great companion for physical pleasure whenever I'd asked, but there has never been any true connection between us. I haven't felt a lasting connection with any of my sexual partners.

I readjust my dress. "Oh this is nothing, don't worry about it." I say it so casually I almost convince myself that I didn't feel a spark when I touched the soft skin of Blythe's shoulder. I can't think about Blythe now though, it's time to get back on track. I don't need any distractions. "Besides, we have a plan." Both our gazes turn toward the heap of stone in the middle of the yard. The Protector Queen. It's more beautiful than I could have imagined, and I can't believe our luck that it's found its way back to Passions Bay after all these years.

Decades before Cece and I were born and Mother was just a child, our great grandmother — The Protector Queen, my pod calls her — used her gift of destruction to carve out a cavern system in the cliffs of Passions Bay, creating a safe home in which our pod can prosper, away from predators and prying human eyes. But one day a human out sailing happened across Great Grandmother, tentacles and all. Instead of being afraid, the human woman was entranced, and so started a great love affair. Before Great Grandmother ended things to marry into a political alliance with a nearby pod, the human woman spent months painstakingly carving a magnificent realistic statue of Great Grandmother in a swirl of mighty tentacles and water. It was a parting gift to signify her everlasting love despite their circumstances.

Years later when Cece and I were just sleeping babes, treasure hunters found and retrieved the statue from the ocean floor outside our caverns after Mother forgot to check the protective illusion wards that make our home invisible to human eyes. It was Mother's first year as Queen, and she took the theft as a personal failure of hers. She hid away from the pod for weeks in her despair. Great Grandmother had passed years earlier, so when her statue disappeared, Mother mourned all over again. On one hand, that incident drove Mother to double down and be the strong, reassuring leader she is today; on the other hand the missing statue remains an open wound.

I look at that same statue now polished and glimmering in the summer sun on dry land. If I didn't know any better, I'd still want it for its striking beauty.

"Your mother will have no choice but to select you as heir once we return The Protector Queen to her," Dom says.

"No choice," I agree.

My gaze is torn from the statue at the sound of Blythe's raspy voice coming through a microphone, filling the yard. My nipples harden beneath my dress at the sound.

"Thank you, Chuck," she says to a cheap Ryan Reynolds knock-off standing beside her. The same knockoff I'd inadvertently spilled champagne all over.

Blythe looks the picture of grace on the outside, but my gift can feel the tension rolling off her. It's strong. Then Not-Ryan wraps an arm around her waist and the emotion intensifies tenfold.

I'm typically a calm person, but anger rocks my body. How dare he make her feel uncomfortable. I want him to take his greasy golden boy hand off her right now. I imagine prying his fingers off her one by one with a clean snap of each one.

Despite it all, Blythe continues, "It's an honor and a privilege to take up residence at Walton Manor following the passing of my amazing grandmother."

The tinge of red clouding my vision clears at that. Grandmother? Blythe is a Walton?

Blythe is a Walton.

Well, shit.

It would have been easy to justify stealing from *The Waltons*, richest business development company in all of Canada. But Blythe didn't strike me as the scummy rich type.

"Keep it together," Dom warns. "We have a plan. This changes nothing."

I've never been good at lying or masking my emotions, so there's no doubt Dom knows exactly what I'm thinking. Damn him.

He's right though. We have a plan. Mission Statue Heist is a go for tomorrow night because I need to do whatever it takes to win that crown. Blythe being the current owner of my family's prized possession doesn't change a thing.

At all.

I hope.

Dom and I spend the rest of the evening mapping out the locations of the security cameras and motion sensors, under the pretense of drinking and mingling. Every now and then I catch Blythe's eye and resist a biological urge to go to her, to help relieve the unease and tension still emanating from her. Though every time our gazes lock, I sense a flicker of something. A mixture of longing, lust, and excitement rolled into one. One look sends the butterflies in my stomach into a frenzy. I genuinely cannot recall a time I've felt that emotion directed at me. When I sleep with other cecaelia back in the pod, they reek of temporary lust, duty, contentedness. Nothing meaningful. Nothing lasting. The idea that I spark excitement and lust in someone has my body humming.

I can tell Dom is getting frustrated the eighth time he has to tell me to focus on the task at hand.

"I am focused," I lie. "I've counted four cameras so far, all with motion sensors."

It wouldn't change anything for him to contradict me even though I'm sure he can smell my desire, but he keeps his mouth shut. Small mercies.

It takes us no longer than an hour to scout the security features, and I'm surprised the property is rather unprotected. The Walton family owns one of the largest real estate development firms in the country, so they're not exactly low profile.

Maybe I should assign some cecaelia to watch over the place? It wouldn't be right to leave the daughter of one of the richest families in America so unprotected.

I shake my head. What am I saying? Blythe is a grown woman who can take care of herself, and I need to focus.

With our scouting mission complete, Dom and I make to head home, but as I round the front of the manor, a wave of fear and annoyance smashes into me, coming from somewhere nearby.

A tinge of my own fear settles in my stomach, and I want more than anything to keep walking.

"What's wrong?" Dom asks, realizing I've fallen out of step with him.

I really do not wish to go toward the emotions. In fact, I wish to curl up in a bed of bubble coral and get a good night's rest after walking in heels all afternoon.

I wish, I wish, I wish.

I also wish to be Queen, and a queen would not walk away from someone in distress.

"One moment," I say. "Stay here."

Dom's muscles tighten, but he does as I command like the obedient bodyguard he is while I follow the emotions, feeling them strengthen as I step through the side entrance into the dark garage.

The second my eyes adjust to the darkness, my body tenses.

Blythe is pinned up against a black SUV. The fear and annoyance ripple off her as Chuck presses his body into hers.

"Babe, calm down and fucking listen to me. I came back here for you and how do you repay me? By avoiding me for half the night and ignoring your guests. How do you think that makes us look?" Chuck enunciates each word with care, a warning lurking behind his calm exterior.

"I didn't ask you to come back," she says, staring him down.

The ice she infuses into her words makes me proud.

Neither of them notice me so I duck behind another vehicle and get as close as I dare. Once I'm crouched behind a wheel, just a couple feet away, I watch.

As backup.

I'm going to give Blythe every chance to fight her own battles, but if that man hurts her in any way, I'm not sure I'll be able to hold back.

"Of course you didn't ask me to come back. And you know why? Because you can be one stubborn bitch, Blythe." He lets out a cruel laugh. "I mean look at this." He pinches the fat on her thigh and gives it a loud slap. "How many times have I said you need to work out? But no, you won't do what I say even if it means respecting your own body."

Blythe winces and a sheen appears in her eyes, but she blinks it back. "Fuck you." Her words come out quiet. "You wouldn't know what respect is if it rammed you up your ass."

That's when it happens. Disgust and anger flares in his eyes.

No. How dare he look at her like that.

Before I know what I'm doing, one of my tentacles shoots out from my dark hiding spot and firmly wraps around his bicep, hopefully cutting off circulation.

"What the f—"

I don't let him finish that thought as I wrench him back by the arm, sending him crashing into the drywall where he crumples like the pathetic waste of sentience he is.

I am not a violent person, but the sound of his head punching a hole in the wall brings me a sick sort of pleasure.

Blythe shrieks and looks around frantically.

I want to go to her, to tell her everything is going to be okay, but I should not even be here right now. I have no business meddling in the affairs of humans. So I stay hidden and watch as she looks between a moaning Chuck and the exit.

Do not go to him, he is not worth it. Please just leave. Please leave, I mentally beg.

After the longest five seconds of my life, Blythe hears my silent plea and rushes from the garage looking around frantically, trying to make sense of what just happened. I want to go to her and tell her it will be okay now. I can't, though.

I stay crouched behind that tire just long enough to ensure I didn't just commit murder in a fit of rage.

When Chuck starts to stir and lets out a pathetic moan of pain, I depart.

CHAPTER FOUR

BLYTHE

As the sun sets, drunk millionaires stumble around the gilded halls of Walton Manor. I no longer have the energy to entertain them. And I sure as hell don't have an ounce of energy to spare for Chuck after he cornered me in the garage and ambushed me with insults, knowing exactly what to say to cut the deepest.

I'm fucking done and need to get out of here, walking ten minutes down a private trail to the main beach, taking up a stranger on her offer of a rendezvous.

Warm ocean water laps at my feet as I wait on a rock for Tabitha.

"I hope that smile is because you're thinking about me," comes a sweet voice.

I look up, my smile widening. "Nah I'm just thinking about this weirdo who crashed my party and hid under a table."

A chilly wind blows off the ocean and Tabitha bites her lip. She's exchanged her slinky gold number for a short t-shirt dress. "About that...If I'd known that was *your* party..."

"What, you'd turn into a pretentious ass-kisser like the rest of my esteemed guests?"

She stands up straighter. "Yes, probably. I suppose it's a good thing you withheld the truth from me." Her lip quirks up at the corner and she looks at me then. "I'm happy you decided to come."

"Me too. This might sound a bit forward, but fuck it: you were the highlight of that party." I brush a blonde lock of hair out of my face. "All afternoon I was fed empty compliments from strangers, listened to people talking about how amazing my ex is, and got called a bitch by said ex."

Tabitha's brows knit together. "Blythe, I'm so sorry." Then, as if a lightbulb appears above her head she says, "Oh speaking of bitches, these are for you." She holds out a bouquet of yellow flowers she'd been hiding behind her back.

Um, did she just call me a bitch?

I tentatively take the insult flowers from her.

She clasps a hand over her mouth then as she realizes what she's just said. "No, no, no. He's the bitch. Not you. You're not a bitch. You're lovely. Sexy, really."

A laugh spills out of me and pink stains her cheeks, highlighting her sharp cheekbones.

She is too fucking cute.

"I grew them myself," she says with a shrug. "They're Black-eyed Susans."

"You grew these? They're beautiful," I gush. I bring the flowers to my face then, inhaling the sweet scent. It's been so long since someone has given me a gift that wasn't an apology or a bribe. Then I notice something in the flowers.

"What's this?" I pluck a little bottle from the middle of the bouquet. "Pepper spray?" I give Tabitha a quizzical look.

She sits down next to me on the rock so that our legs are touching.

"In case you need to use it on knockoff Ryan Reynolds." She says it so sweetly, all embarrassment gone, that it takes a second for me to grasp her meaning. Then I burst out laughing all over again. The thought of pepper spraying that smug grin off Chuck's botoxed face makes me snort.

When I finally catch my breath, I have to ask, "Oh god, was it that obvious I can't stand him?"

"No, you put up a good front, but I have a second sense with these things." She winks, sending my heart into superspeed. "Sometimes guys like that need a strong hand to teach them how to behave. It's part of the reason my mother had me trained to defend myself."

I look her up and down — this five-foot nothing water sprite of a woman — and cock a brow.

"You don't believe me, do you?" She pouts.

"Show me," I challenge.

"Stand up."

I do as she says and we move away from the rocks into the fluffy sand.

"Now attack me," she says.

"Wait, what? No!"

"Just do it, I promise you won't hurt me!" She laughs.

I've never attacked anyone in my life, so I do the next best thing and run at her like I'm meeting her at the airport after years apart and I'm going to envelop her in a bear hug. However, my arms never connect because Tabitha flips me over her shoulder and the world spins. My back gently meets the sand and Tabitha's warm body is on top of mine, straddling me, pinning my arms above my head. I can feel my maxi dress bunched around my waist.

We look at each other for a second, taking in our intimate position.

She's more devious than she lets on; this was totally planned.

Tabitha tucks a strand of hair behind her ear shyly. "I learned lots of stuff like that."

"Kiss me."

She stops talking, mouth forming an *O*, and I realize I said that out loud. So I say it again because fuck, I want her to kiss me. That's not even the full truth because what I really want is to taste if her dripping cunt is as salty as the ocean, to feel her writhe in pleasure at the mercy of my touch.

"It would be my pleasure, Blythe," she says.

She cups my face, her long black nails grazing my ears, and brings her lips to mine. The second our lips connect, I'm flooded with a sense of warmth and comfort, of passion and fire, of everything good I've been without my whole life. Tabitha is soft and tender, and I need more of her. I need more of this tiny woman who was thoughtful enough to hide from my ex with me and randomly gift me some means of protection and safety. I don't know who she is or if she's even looking for a relationship, but if this is all I get of her, I'm going to make it count.

I wrap my arms around her and pull her closer, so our bodies are pressed together. Her heart is just as erratic as mine. I slip my tongue between her pouty lips and the intoxicating taste of saltwater floods my senses.

"Tabitha," I breathe.

Her hands trail their way down my body. "Tell me to stop whenever you want, and I will."

"There's no fucking chance," I say.

She smiles against my lips as her hand makes a beeline for my cunt, slipping under my panties.

"Blythe Walton, you are so wet for me," she purrs, all pretense of innocence gone. Her fingers brush along my slick folds before plunging into me.

I let out a gasp and squeeze my legs together.

Then she brings those fingers to her mouth and sucks, like she's experiencing pure ecstasy. "Darling, you are by far the best dessert I've had tonight." She plunges a finger into me again before pulling out and suddenly I'm tasting myself on her fingers in my mouth. "See how sweet you are."

My head spins as I suck at her fingers, swirling my tongue around to eat up every last drop.

This confident seductress is completely different from the awkwardly adorable woman at the party, but I don't care. I'm liking both sides of her just fine.

"More please," I whimper when she removes her fingers from my mouth.

She flashes a wicked grin. "It's my turn now, I'm famished."

In one fluid motion, she slides off me and hoists my legs over her shoulders, bringing my pussy right to her pillowy lips.

I gasp at the contact and my mind swims. If I could think straight, I might wonder how the hell such a tiny person could lift me with such ease, but all I can think about is her mouth on my pussy.

I moan in pleasure as her hot tongue circles my entrance slowly, teasing me. I start rocking my hips, needing more and she obliges, plunging her tongue inside. She sets a rhythm in and out that has me writhing beneath her, helpless.

Holy fucking shit.

When was the last time I'd felt a pleasure this intense? In my recollection, never.

Tabitha squeezes my ass as she drags her tongue over my folds in one all-encompassing lick and I buck at the jolt of heat that shoots through my body.

Her grip on me tightens. "I'm not done yet, darling. I wonder what would happen if I did this."

Another jolt of heat shoots through me as she flicks her tongue over my sensitive clit.

"I love how you squirm for me," she says, and does it again. And again. And again.

I squeeze my legs tight around her head as the pressure builds inside me. I'm about to explode when my attention is abruptly yanked away by the feeling of something slithering around my wrist.

What.

The.

Fuck.

I shriek and rip myself away from Tabitha, slapping at my arm.

"What's going on?" Tabitha jumps up, my panic mimicked on her face.

"There was—" What was there? Looking around now, we're all alone on the beach in the moonlight, save for a little yellow crab dancing like he's trying to make sandy crop circles. "—something, there was something on my arm. Like a snake, but maybe not..." I know I sound like a paranoid mess right now. After all, there's nothing here. Could it have been my imagination?

Tabitha's face turns ghostly white.

I rush over to her. "Oh my god, your face. Are you afraid of snakes?"

"Sorry, I have to go," she mutters.

"I'm sorry," I try, but the words die off in the breeze.

Tabitha, however, isn't headed up the beach towards the parking lot or the main strip. She's broken out into a run for the cliffs. I watch in concern as she wades into the waist-deep water and disappears behind the rocks. It takes a minute before common sense kicks in and then I'm running after her, calling her name. I splash into the surf, my Saint Laurent maxi dress getting destroyed in the process. I round the edge of the cliff and am greeted with gentle waves and the moonlight on the water's surface. Tabitha is gone.

Chapter Five

TABITHA

I'd been avoiding Dom all day, putting off the inevitable lecture I'll get for inciting the local police to snoop around the cliffs. Even though we have a protective ward around the entrances of our home, it's best to be as incognito as possible to avoid accidental discovery. Thankfully, none of my people care enough about human affairs to wonder why the police were in the area.

I got lucky.

I should have known that Blythe would call emergency services when I'd disappeared into the water at the rocky cliffs, but I wasn't thinking straight at the time. She got in my head, and I'd completely lost control of my body and almost revealed my cecaelia form to her. Luckily she just thought my tentacle was a snake. I tell myself that I'm not gaslighting her, I'm just preserving my people, but I still feel like a bad person.

I toe the wet sand with my human foot and hug my black hoodie to myself, bracing for a lecture as Dom's footsteps near.

My bodyguard rounds the corner of the cliff, dressed in black in his human form, looking chuffed. He drops a full duffle bag at my feet. "Are you ready to go, Princess?"

I nod, choosing not to comment on his use of my formal title. If he's going to ignore my earlier indiscretion, great.

He grunts, pulling out a smaller backpack full of supplies and hands it to me. "Do you remember the plan?"

He's avoiding my gaze. Maybe I deserve it, but I still hate it.

"I remember the plan."

"Good, let's get in and out as quickly as possible."

We make our way from the beach to Walton Manor under the cover of a moonless night in an uncomfortable silence.

Dom and I circle the massive property at a safe distance and don't see anyone.

Good.

He unzips my backpack and retrieves a can of silicone spray, which he plants in my hand. "I'll keep a look out. Be quick and stay safe," he says in his low *I-mean-business* tone.

We split up and I pick my way toward the beautiful three-story Tudor-style manor, making sure to stay in the security camera dead zones. As I approach the garden lining the house, I shift into my cecaelia form, eight tentacles erupting from my body, adding a few extra inches to my height. In this form, I easily crawl over a rosebush to latch a tentacle onto one of the many vines snaking their way up the house.

My heart jumps into my throat as I look up. I'm not exactly afraid of heights but living mostly in the ocean and in caves does give one an aversion to high up places.

I take a deep breath and give the vine a tug. I'm relieved to find it holds solid. Ignoring the voice in my head yelling at me to stay on the ground, I rear back and push off my back tentacles, catching myself like a spider monkey against the side of the house. With eight tentacles and two arms, I have no problem scaling the wall until I get to the motion sensor light aimed at The Protector Queen statue.

Holy moly, that is a long way down.

I close my eyes for a beat, then hold the spray can to the sensor just as a light flicks on in my peripheral vision. Curious, I crawl to the window in question and peer in. Through the sheer curtain I can make out Blythe with her body wrapped in a towel, coming out of a bathroom. Before I even register my brain telling me to look away and give her privacy, her towel drops to the floor and my jaw drops open. Through the gauzy fabric of the curtain, I can still see everything. The way her full thighs pull into adorable hip dimples, the soft curve of her stomach leading up to a swell of full perky breasts, her little nose that peaks up just a little at the tip.

I look away quickly, breath suddenly heavy.

What am I doing? I'm not some creepy peeping tom, nor am I genuinely attracted to a human. I'm not.

I force myself back to the motion sensor light and coat the entire thing in a silicone spray to jam the connection, then carefully crawl back down the wall, taking great care to avoid Blythe's window.

As my tentacles touch down on the gloriously safe ground, I spot Dom by the pool shed and give him a nod.

Phase one complete.

Still avoiding the cameras, I meet Dom at the pool shed.

He wrinkles his nose at me and curses under his breath. "I can smell your arousal from here, and it's not for me. You need to stifle whatever this thing is between you and that human now before it ruins everything."

My body goes stiff and before I can stop them, the words are out of my mouth, "I am your princess and you will show me respect. You will not so much as speak of Blythe while you are in my presence. That is an order, Dominic." My voice is stern and uncompromising. Is this what it means to be Queen?

Dom flinches at my words, then seems to recover. A muscle works furiously in his jaw, then he finally mutters, "Yes, Princess."

I don't have time to feel bad about pulling rank like that because we need to move.

We follow the dead zones from around the shed to behind a hedge, and over to our target: The Protector Queen.

She looks so out of place in the middle of the empty expanse of yard. We'll bring her home to her rightful place, surrounded by cecaelia.

Dom tosses a strap to me. "Here, secure the statue around the base." Using his gift of strength, he easily lifts the statue for me to wrap the straps under and around, creating a makeshift strappy statue backpack for him to carry. In one big hoist, we have the statue secured on his back, ready to go. We both have all tentacles out to help balance the load so it doesn't start tipping, when a floodlight switches on.

Dom and I freeze.

Blythe stands barefoot on the cobbled patio in a light dressing gown, hair still wet, mouth agape. She's absolutely repulsed.

I have a million excuses on my tongue to try and explain Dom's strength, our tentacles, our theft, but there's absolutely nothing I can say that would make any of this okay. My heart breaks at the way she's looking at me right now, and I instinctively know she's wearing her contacts. She can see everything, and I'm helpless to do anything about it.

"Hey, thieves!" Chuck calls after us, stomping out of the kitchen, looking non-threatening in a pair of tighty whities, squinting without his glasses on. "I have the police on the phone now! You lot won't get away with this! Do you know who you're stealing from?

Blythe is silent and doesn't make a move.

"Tabby, we have to go, we'll deal with her later," Dom says.

Deal with her later, like she's just some problem to fix.

Sirens blare to life in the distance, and I know Dom's right. We have to go. Now.

I shoot Blythe one final look that I hope conveys the depth of the apology stirring in my heart, then Dom and I disappear over the hill and into the water.

CHAPTER SIX

BLYTHE

I give a twirl in the baby yellow Claire McCardell sundress I'd found while cleaning out Grandmother's closet. It must have belonged to my great grandmother when she'd lived here back in the day. The cross-wrapped halter neck tying off into a fluffy bow at the back of my neck still works today. It's a fun and classy dress — one I'm going to wear out once Chuck leaves. Though at this point the notion of Chuck leaving is just as likely as the idea of me and Tabitha being together.

I feel a confusing twinge in my heart at the thought of her. My gut is telling me to give her the benefit of the doubt, but the bottom line is that she was just using me to pass the time until she could steal from me.

I know, I know, rich girl problems.

It still fucking sucks.

I change out of Great Grandmother's dress and stare at it on the hanger. She could have been wearing that exact dress when she fell in love with the cecaelia queen. I shove it in a bin destined for the attic.

My grandmother had always insisted on the story of my great grandmother falling in love with the cecaelia being true, but nobody ever took her story seriously.

I tip my head back and rapidly blink away the moisture building there.

Sorry it took a while, but I'm taking you seriously now Great Grandmother. But how you could love such dishonest creatures is beyond me.

Cleaning out Grandma's closet was supposed to be a distraction from what I'd seen last night and from Chuck's current security bender, hiring crews to set up motion detectors, more cameras, even hiring a live-in guard. I didn't get a wink of sleep last night. That tends to happen when the world as you knew it is so completely disrupted. Cecaelia? Really? I wish I could blame what I saw last night on alcohol or sleeping pills, but I know what I saw.

I feel a pop and look down to see an old linen shirt pulled taut in my hands, and one of its buttons now beside my foot.

Shit. I can't stop thinking about it.

I abandon my failed clean up job and head to my bedroom grabbing the Black-eyed Susans still in their bouquet next to my bed. But before I can even think about stomping downstairs and tossing them out the front door, a figure steps out in front of me, his broad chest blocking my path.

I take an involuntary step back.

"What are those?" Chuck barges in looking abnormally sweaty for someone just ordering everyone around outside.

"Flowers," I say.

"I'm not an imbecile darling. Who gave them to you?"

Here we go. "Just a neighbour from the garden party. A Mrs. Hartman or Horton."

Chuck frowns and stalks closer.

"I know when you're lying, you always shake your head a little, like you know you're a lying bitch too. So? Who the fuck is he?" His voice grows louder as unchecked emotions bleed from him.

"There's no *him*, Chuck." True. "And it wouldn't matter if there were because this," I gesture between us, "is over. It's not a thing anymore."

Chuck has the audacity to laugh and run a hand through his hair. "Oh Blythe, grow up. Everybody cheats and it means nothing. Once this temper tantrum of yours is over, you'll realize you will never do better than me, and we'll go back home to Toronto."

My blood boils at the condescension dripping from his smug face. I don't trust myself to open my mouth so I try to shove past him but he steps in my way like some lunchtime bully.

"Blythe, calm—"

"Get the fuck out," I snap. "I want you out. You're trespassing now. Out." I point to the door but he doesn't budge.

His face hardens and he grips my shoulders a little too tight. "Quit being a spoiled bitch so we can talk about this."

Bitch. He called me a *bitch*. Again.

I try and wriggle out of his grip, but he holds tight. "Let go, you're hurting me."

"You're fine, just fucking stop for a second," he growls.

When I can't get free, my body reacts all on its own as I reach into the bouquet and find purchase on that tiny bottle I'd left there, the perfect hiding place from Chuck. I didn't think I'd ever actually use it on him. It was more of a security blanket than anything.

Shock and fear register on Chuck's face just as I press the nozzle and pepper spray erupts from the can.

Chuck releases me and falls to his knees, clutching his face, bellowing like an injured cat. Behind him panting in the doorway is Tabitha.

Tabitha in a sandy rough spun dress, hair still dripping water, and on two legs.

"Are you okay? I heard a scream." She's out of breath, like she ran here. Then she takes in the scene and a smile starts to creep onto her face. But she's not the good guy here.

I train the pepper spray on her next. "You're either brave or incredibly stupid for showing your face here again. I know what you are." *Party crasher. Thief. Liar.*

Tabitha slowly steps into the room, hands raised in innocence. "Yes, I'm a cecaelia — an octopus person." She steels herself. "And I won't apologize for who I am."

I roll my eyes. "I don't care that you're a cecaelia — it's the lying and stealing and using me that I can't forgive. You know, after that party I really thought you might be a half-decent person who would never use me for my money." I throw my arms up. "But hey way to prove me wrong. Go big or go home, right? How much did your buyer promise you for it? A few million?" My tone goes sarcastic then. "Because it's worth at least ten million — I don't want you to get ripped off or anything." My voice catches and I stop talking. I will not cry in front of my ex and my...nothing. Tabitha is my nothing.

Tabitha slowly approaches me like I'm a feral cat she's trying not to spook.

Fuck this.

I go to spray the can but a tentacle whips out inhumanly fast and halts my finger.

We both stare at her tentacle on my hand and she quickly pulls it away, wringing the limb in her hands in embarrassment. "I'm sorry, but you don't seem that surprised or scared about...all this." With a flourish of her hand, seven more lavender tentacles sprout from beneath her dress, slinking down to the floor and lifting Tabitha taller. Each appendage is thick as thighs near her waist, then taper off into elegantly slim tips. I almost miss it, but when Tabitha shifts on her tentacles, I notice the way her suckers undulate, like they're moving with an invisible current. Then her human legs simply vanish, as if they'd never been there.

"So? Please tell me what you're thinking."

It takes a conscious effort to keep my mouth from dropping open. It's one thing to have heard stories about them and to have seen them from a distance at night, but this... This little water pixie of a woman has transformed into a strong sea witch in front of my eyes. She's magnificent.

No, she's a liar.

I remember then that she's waiting for me to respond, so I shake my head and toss the pepper spray on the bed. Chuck is still blind on the floor, wailing. So I gather the neck of his shirt in my fist and shove him out the door, locking it behind him. Locking Tabitha and I in together.

She keeps her distance. She might not be the enemy Chuck is, but she's still definitely not a friend.

The bed moans as I slump onto it, suddenly exhausted.

Tabitha waits respectfully by the door.

"I was told stories of cecaelia growing up, though I didn't believe them until now. So thank you for trying to ensure I remained an ignorant human. I really appreciate looking like an idiot." Damn, I can't stop with the sarcasm. "Oh and getting close to me so I wouldn't suspect anything after letting slip you were crashing my party? Brilliant. Truly, Tabitha, hats off to you."

"Blythe, it's not like—"

"Oh and that statue you stole? I don't even care about the money part of it. I didn't think I was ever going to see it after it was auctioned off years ago, but I just got that piece of my family history back. I had it for all of twenty-four hours before a couple of fucking sea witches stole it. Did you know that my great grandmother sculpted it herself, by hand?

Tabitha's eyes widen.

So she didn't know that part then.

I continue, "It was a portrait of the love of her life —"

"My great grandmother," Tabitha finishes.

"Your..." Goosebumps prickle my skin as I realize what she's telling me. My great grandmother sculpted that statue for the cecaelia queen — who is real. Which means..."

"You're a royal?"

"That's my family heirloom," we say in unison.

My cheeks flush with heat and I slump to the floor, burying my face in my hands. The adrenaline leaves my body in one big rush.

"I'm such an idiot!" I shout into my palms. "I almost fucking pepper sprayed you because you were trying to steal back a family artifact."

"Hey, hey stop that." Tabitha sits down next to me with her back against the bed, her tentacles gone now, and wraps an arm around me. "You're not an idiot. You're a wonderful, reasonable human who didn't know the full story." She delicately tucks a strand of hair behind my ear. "Speaking of the full story, are you okay?" She gestures to the can of pepper spray, and I choke out a laugh.

"Ya, I told him to leave and he refused."

A brilliant grin breaks across her face. "I'm so proud of you for standing up for yourself and for putting him in his place. I wanted to do the same thing to him when you gave the speech at your garden party.

I turn to her. "Did you now? And why, pray tell, is that?".

"Actually that's what I came here to tell you — after explaining myself and hoping you weren't going to call one of those new security guys on me — I really like you, Blythe. You're funny and so effortlessly charming. You make me want to actually leave my books and have some fun. I just... I guess I wanted to formally ask for your forgiveness for not telling you the truth about me earlier. Then I wanted to ask you on a date — pending the apology acceptance of course."

She sounds so dorky and adorable and the words are out of my mouth before I can think them: "Of course I forgive you." I nudge her foot with mine.

Then eight tentacles sprout from beneath her dress and her legs disappear. "And would you consider going on a date with a monster?"

I look her up and down. "If you can explain how you did that and promise to keep me in the know... then yes."

She lets out a happy gasp as I throw my arms around her in a hug, the force sending us both falling sideways onto the floor, giggling.

"So, when do I get to meet the fam?" I joke.

CHAPTER SEVEN

TABITHA

The place is packed with cecaelia mingling and grazing on crab cakes and clam dip. The classical music of a string quartet fills the space with the class and elegance that's near impossible to pull off in a damp cavern, but of course Mother made it happen.

After reconciling with Blythe, I had the most life changing month of my life. One completely normal date at a human seafood restaurant led to another, which led to Blythe and me being inseparable for weeks. I learned how she recently left her role as curator of a private art gallery and sold her stock in her family's corporation as a means of cutting ties from Chuck and starting over. Since then, we've been trying to find her passion. Together. Lucky for me that meant paint nights, surf lessons, trips to the local museum, and we have so much more planned. Blyth has opened my eyes to the world and all it has to offer outside of my pod.

After dozens of arguments with Dom and tearful conversations with Blythe, I came to the decision to forfeit my royal title. A life as Pod Queen would mean devoting my life to my pod. There'd be no room for humans in my life. Not even one. Even if Blythe and I didn't work out in the end, I wanted to move to a space with more sunlight to grow my plants and wanted to travel to see human conferences on climate action. That life wouldn't be possible for Queen Tabitha. So I hadn't planned on attending Mother's fiftieth birthday eve soiree. But Blythe insisted.

I give her hand a squeeze as we navigate through the crowd and find a shadowed table in the back.

"This is incredible," she whispers. Her eyes sparkle as she takes in some partygoers in their naked cecaelia form.

I was thinking the same thing about her, in her emerald green mermaid dress that shows off the addicting dip of her back and curve of her hips. Her hair is still dripping wet from our trip through the water tunnel system and dark green trails bead down her dress from the water.

"You're incredible," I whisper, leaning in for a kiss.

In readjusting to get closer to her, I accidentally kick the scuba apparatus under the table with my heals. The sound rings through the echoey room and all heads turn to us.

"Sorry," I mouth.

Blythe is shaking beside me, trying so hard not to laugh.

I'm saved from further embarrassment as Mother takes the stage to give her speech, chin tipped up, waiting patiently for the pod to quiet themselves.

Of course, she expressed confusion and disappointment at my decision to drop out of the running for the crown and did her best to convince me to reconsider, but I know what I want. *Who* I want.

Besides, once I presented her with The Protector Queen, she broke down in tears and gave me her blessing to go off and live the life that would make me happy. I intend to do just that.

Now she turns to my twin on stage who has secured a non-marital alliance with another pod. Interesting. Pride radiates off Mother so much I'm sure everyone else can feel it too, as she crowns a beaming Cece, the next queen.

Blythe pulls me aside to check in, and I feel relieved to have a brief moment alone.

"I'm really okay with this," I promise. "More than okay. This is what I want." I plant a peck on her lips and a wicked look crosses her face.

Before I know it, Blythe tugs me into a dark adjacent room used for storage, throws shut the curtain, and erases the distance between us. She pins me up against the wall, her toned thigh wedged between my legs, and her full, sugary sweet lips on mine. I have never felt such a fire with someone before and I don't want it to end. I kiss her back with the intensity I feel in return and she smiles against my mouth.

"I've wanted to do this ever since I first met you," she breathes.

"Do what?" I ask.

"Feast on you with people less than five feet away." She smirks. "May I?"

Her body sinks lower and I find that I'm completely incapable of saying no. That word isn't a part of my vocabulary anymore. "Please," I say.

If this past month has taught me anything, it's that it doesn't matter how many limbs you have. How you use them is what really counts. And my gorgeous four-limbed human is a master of her craft. Blythe's tongue meets my center and I see stars.

I let out a moan of pleasure as eight tentacles sprout from me involuntarily, replacing my legs.

Blythe's eyes widen in surprise and delight.

Up until now, I've held off being fully in my cecaelia form during sex, only bringing out one tentacle here and there to spice things up.

I'm about to shift back to human when I feel teeth gently grazing my throbbing clit. "Don't you dare change, Tabby," she says against me.

I don't need any more convincing than that.

Blythe redoubles her efforts, a slender manicured finger plunging into me as her tongue expertly teases me.

Release comes quickly as a blinding wave rocks through my body. I ride Blythe's face as the blissful shutters rock through me and I want nothing more than to stay here forever with my human.

It isn't until I look down that I realize I forgot to warn her.

Her face is covered in the black ink from my orgasm, the substance dripping from her chin and into her cleavage.

I'm about to apologize when her tongue circles her lips, cleaning me off her face, and she smiles.

"Thank you." She looks up at me with reverence in her eyes. "I've never tasted a cecaelia before."

I pick her up in my tentacles then, earning a delighted shriek of surprise.

"Darling, you will never taste another cecaelia for as long as I live. You are all mine and only mine."

Absolute delight crosses her face. "Only yours, tentacle mommy," she agrees.

A shiver of desire rolls up my spine at the sound of her new nickname for me. "Yes, I like that. As your tentacle mommy, I'll take you to the brink and make sure you're fully satisfied. Tell me to stop whenever you want and I will," I echo the same sentiment I offer to her every time.

A gleam of mischief flashes in her eyes. "Not a chance. Show me everything you've got. Nothing is off limits."

I have heard humans call my kind in fiction *sea witches* or *demons of the deep*, but I'm not the wicked one between us right now.

"Are you sure you know what you're asking for, Blythe? I don't want to hurt you."

She leans up and gives me the most tender kiss. "I'll let you know if it's too much. I promise."

I love you, I want to say. But now is not the time.

Prepare to experience the full extent of a former cecaelia princess.

With a wink, I splay my human out like a starfish against the wall, a tentacle pinning each limb in place, off the floor.

"Wait," she pants. "What about my dress? I need it to walk out of here."

"The dress isn't a problem," I rasp. I slip two tentacles down the neckline of her dress, wrap around the soft warm skin of her breasts, heaving them out of their fabric prison so they're on display. Her nipples are already pebbled into perfect pink peaks for me.

"I'm going to fuck you so hard, you won't be able to think or walk straight for weeks. But don't worry, I'll take care of you in the meantime."

"Oh I can handle you, Tabby. Just try me."

The nervous bravery radiating from my ridiculously sexy human is everything.

All at once I put three tentacles to work, fixing the suction cups of two tentacles to Blythe's hardened nipples and sucking, at the same time I plunge a third appendage inside her tight little pussy that's never experienced the full width of a tentacle before.

A happy scream explodes from her and I quickly shove a tentacle into her mouth too to keep her quiet.

"Do you want to know a fun fact?" I whisper in her ear.

She makes a sound around my tentacle.

"Did you know that cecaelia are at the top of the food chain in the ocean? And the suckers on a cecaelia's tentacles can taste things even better than our tongues can."

Her eyes widen and I push just a little deeper into her tight pussy that's threatening to cut off my circulation.

"And fuck darling, I can't get enough of your sweet taste."

The vibrations of her unintelligible words around my tentacle send hot tingles down my spine.

Addicting. Delicious. Perfect. "I want you to be my exclusive scent."

She lets out a happy moan. That addicting sound. I want to hear more of it.

"Oh look, I still have one more tentacle," I say, curling the tip under her chin. "Brace yourself, darling."

As I continue a steady rhythm in and out of Blythe's pussy and mouth, I slither my last tentacle up her leg and nudge at the bud of her ass.

She lets out a shudder and nods, her eyes pleading.

This time, I enter her slowly, giving her every chance to tell me no. But she doesn't.

She's so tight I'm afraid I might hurt her, but she slowly opens up for me. When she's taken a mind boggling five inches of me in her ass, another moan spills from her lips. Fuck, those vibrations.

I become feral, a wild thing.

Her ass, pussy, mouth, tits, they're all mine.

She's mine.

With one final suck at her nipples and plunge into every orifice, my brave little starfish comes undone around me, a hot release squirting out from her, soaking my tentacles in her juices.

EPILOGUE: BLYTHE

"Do you need a hand?" I poke my head in the master bedroom of Walton Manor where Tabby is filling our closet with the rest of her clothes, which honestly isn't much. It turns out that cecaelia are usually naked, so everything she owns is either for special events or for blending in with humans. I've topped up her closet a bit over the past couple of months, but old habits die hard for her.

"Nope, I am just about done," she says, putting up the final hanger. "You know, it's a good thing I don't have many clothes because you didn't make a ton of space for me in here," she teases.

I come up behind her and wrap my arms around her neck, planting a kiss on her cheek. "Oh but you make up for it with all the plants you brought here!" I point out. "Speaking of which, I have a surprise for you. Do you have a sec?"

Tabby squints her eyes in adorable mock-skepticism but follows anyway.

It's been a couple months since Tabby rescinded her claim to the throne. Something I don't think I'll ever be able to repay her for, though I'll sure as hell do my best. It took a little while but after a few strategic phone calls I was able to pull together human identities for Tabby and Dom, complete with fake birth records, identification, credit cards, everything any human would need to survive on land. Even though I left the family business, I still have plenty of contacts in high up places. Since that all came together last week, the love of my life and her bodyguard have officially moved into Walton Manor.

Dom really takes his job seriously. Princess, Queen, cecaelia-living-on-land, it doesn't matter to him. His duty is still to Tabby. He isn't the biggest fan of humans, but I think he's started warming up to me ever since I gave him free reign and the funds to fully equip the manor in whatever security features his sassy little heart desired.

"Now close your eyes," I say, leading Tabby by the hand, out into the backyard. "Remember when you literally gave up your entire life to be with some random woman you'd only known for a few weeks?"

She snorts and I can practically feel her eyeroll. "I think I remember something like that. Do you recall how you let go of all the staff at Walton Manor so you could house two monsters of the deep?"

"It was the least I could do! Those things aren't even comparable," I laugh, skirting a rose bush. "I'm sure I can figure out how to cook something without a chef. If not, there's always restaurants, frozen foods, subscription boxes, and I know you've got the seafood thing covered. So maybe I don't even need to learn to cook," I muse. "Okay, okay, we're here." I can't keep the excitement from bleeding out of me, not that I'd be able to hide it from Tabby's gift anyway. "Open your eyes, my love."

Tabby's eyes flutter open in the midafternoon sun and pure happiness fills her whole person at the sight.

"Blythe, wha—" she starts. "I mean, how? When did this get here? Is it all for me?" She is in awe at the magnificent greenhouse I had installed for her.

"It's all just for you," I squeal. I cannot keep my cool about this. She is going to lose her mind even more in a minute. "Come on, let me show you inside."

I throw open the double glass doors and we're welcomed with the heady scent of earth and florals. Tabby takes a deep breath and even though I don't have her gift, I can see all her worries about living on land melting away.

I give her the grand tour, showing her the plants she'd brought with her from her cavern and even more I just thought she might like, explaining how I hired horticulturists to make sure everything was done just right. From the hanging planters, to the rows of perennials and annuals, the fruits, vegetables... it's a horticulturalist's wet dream.

"What's this?" she asks, tapping her knuckle against a frosted glass room. "I could feel your excitement building the closer we got to here so...?" She raises her brows, still beaming from our tour.

"This is the *pièce de résistance*! Behold," I say and swing the door open to reveal tanks upon tanks of Tabby's thriving seagrass.

I strive over to a desk where a single piece of paper lay and hold it out to her.

She takes it and reads it over, her eyes growing wide. "Blythe, are you saying... This is real?"

I bite my lip and nod.

"Blythe!" she screams and performs a running jump into my arms, her tentacles sprouting out of her to wrap me in the most suffocatingly brilliant hug I've ever experienced. I spin us around, laughing and kissing her.

Right after Tabby had told me about the prototype for a sea-grass-based plastic alternative that she perfected last month, I knew exactly what I had to do next.

"So," I say once I've put Tabby down, "the patent is good for plastic alternatives with a base made from any type of seagrass. It's real. You did it, and the idea is officially and exclusively yours."

"Blythe, I don't know what to say," she says, hurrying over to the tank to check the thermometers in the water and feel the emotions of the seagrass. She's such a nerd and I love it.

"Just say you'll marry me."

She spins around to see me on one knee, box open in my hand to display a teardrop shaped emerald set into a delicate white gold band.

"Tabitha, you have given up your life as you knew it to start a new life with me and I intend to make you the happiest woman in the world. Together, we're going to make history, I know it. Starting with a wedding, if you'll have me. Then maybe we'll work together to solve the world plastics crisis."

A laugh bubbles out of her as the tears rimming her eyes sparkle against the sun filtering into the greenhouse. "Blythe—" she starts to say when Dom barges in.

"Hey guys, when the hell did we get a greenhou—" He halts abruptly in the doorway and presses his lips together taking in the scene.

We all just stare at each other for a minute.

Then he slowly reaches into his jeans pocket and pulls out a phone, holding it up to record us.

Damn, I should have thought to record this. I guess I can't be mad at him now.

"Blythe," Tabby says, helping me up with a tentacle, "it would be my honor."

THE END

SEDUCING THE CECAELIA BODYGUARD

MAY MATTHEWS

CHAPTER ONE

DOMINIC

Overenthusiastic whoops and cheers echo off the marble walls of the hotel lobby as a group of women clad in pink and gold phallic merchandise stumble for the elevator.

I scan the space for a sober chaperone. A white-gloved bellhop rolls a suitcase laden cart to a small service elevator off to the side while a large fountain with a stone mermaid at its center spews a stream of water into its teal pool full of assorted coins. But once the elevator doors close and the trickle of water is the only sound remaining, I realize there isn't a chaperone. Unescorted and drunken in public. Completely vulnerable and under the influence.

I shake my head. That was one difference I'd quickly picked up between humans and cecaelia. Humans didn't think twice about roaming under the influence in public where anything could happen to them. Cecaelia weren't that blind to their own mortality. If a cecaelia were to swim out of the caverns without their wits about them, they could easily get caught in a swarm of jellyfish or stumble into the path of a confused great white. But the biggest threat? Everyone knows it's humans you need to stay away from. Humans, albeit unfathomably idiotic at times, are the apex predator.

I check my watch for the hundredth time and sigh loudly. The receptionist is straining his eyes looking much too intently at his computer, doing his best not to acknowledge me.

My phone pings with an incoming text message from the reason I'm here.

Tabby: *Did you sign it yet??*

Last night, Tabby and Blythe convinced me to come here for them as a favour. After Blythe's attempt at cooking oysters, both she and Tabby were holed up in their restrooms for the rest of the night and into this morning. That's when they got an email about a cancellation at this beachside resort wedding venue. Naturally they needed to tour and accept the venue in-person today or else it would have gone to the next couple on the waiting list. That's how I ended up sitting on this stiff crème couch for an hour, waiting on the wedding coordinator to get her head out of her ass to come get this thing over with so I can get back to Tabby's side.

Before I left this morning, I'd double-checked the security system and I'm confident they won't be leaving the property — hell, they won't be leaving their golden thrones. But I'll still feel much better when I'm by her side again. A bodyguard's habits die hard.

I respond quickly.

Dominic: *No. Still waiting.*

Tabby: *Okay, keep me posted! And do not decapitate the coordinator for their lack of punctuality. We need them in one piece for the wedding.*

Dominic: *Mhm.*

Fuck this.

I stand, readjusting my pressed black jacket and black dress pants that are creased from the three hour drive here, courtesy of one of Blythe's old drivers, and head for the receptionist who's cowering behind his monitor.

But my progress is interrupted as someone rushes face-first into my side. They ricochet off me like a bumper car hitting a semi-truck.

"I'm so sorry, sir!" a five foot nothing woman sings before twisting back around and stepping up to the counter. She couldn't be more than twenty-five years old, with her round face, headphones hanging around her neck, and a backpack slouched over her shoulder.

The receptionist's shoulders relax slightly as he shoots me a glance around the woman.

"Lovely day today, sir. I sure hope your shift is done soon so you can enjoy it. Now, do you happen to have a restroom I can use?" she asks.

"I'm sorry ma'am, restrooms are for paying guests only. Would you like me to book you in?"

She looks around at the grandeur of the place, her red curls bouncing with each cock of her head. When she's fully assessed this place to be far too expensive for her, she turns back to the receptionist and lowers her voice, "Please sir, this is kind of an emergency. I'll be real quick and won't tell anyone you let me in."

I don't get to see the thrilling conclusion to their exchange because it's then that a severe looking woman in a smart navy suit calls out, "Tabitha and Blythe?"

Finally.

I raise a hand and march over to her. "That would be me." Then I add, "Your eleven o'clock."

She looks me up and down with a pinched expression. "I'm sorry, I think there's been a misunderstanding. This appointment is scheduled for Tabitha and Blythe. No stand-ins will be tolerated, you understand. This is a highly sought after venue and if the wedding couple is not present, I'll have no choice but to reach out to the next couple on the waiting list. So can we expect them to be joining us, sir?"

Well, that's bullshit.

I open my mouth to respond and quickly shut it again before I let my sarcasm get the better of me. I can't let the venue of my best friend's dreams slip through my fingers because of some bullshit policy. I clear my throat and look at her nametag. "Listen Marge, you're going to give me this tour. You've kept me waiting for an hour — an hour I'll never get back. So I expect—"

"Whoops, I'm sorry about that ma'am. My name's Tabitha," the red-haired woman calls as she bounces over and wraps her hands around my arm, pressing herself into my side.

I stiffen at the touch of this stranger.

She can't be more than half my size and is deliciously thick. My sightline straight down her ample cleavage has me instantly thinking things I don't want to think about any human. My cock twitches as her coconut scent fills my senses and I have to look away from her.

What the fuck was that? I don't react this way to humans. Ever.

"I was just speaking with your lovely concierge, looking for a restroom," the woman continues. "Would you be able to direct me before we get started?" The lie rolls off her tongue so sweet and so easily.

"Of course, right this way," Marge says, narrowing her eyes at me before leading us further into the resort.

As soon as her back is to us, I shake the woman off my arm. I need personal space.

She smirks and releases me. "You're welcome," she mouths as if she's done me a huge favour. I didn't ask for her help, so I don't indulge her with a response.

"This is our grand ballroom," Marge announces as we enter an immense space of marble floors, white walls with intricate moulding, and chandeliers dripping in crystals. But its focal point is a wall of floor to ceiling windows overlooking the ocean. My home.

I have to hand it to Tabby and Blythe, they have good taste. As cecaelia, Tabby and I find comfort in being close to the ocean where we'd spent most of our lives. Moving onto land to live with Tabby's fiancé had been an adjustment that was only bearable since Blythe's manor was an oceanfront property.

"We are behind schedule," Marge says, voice echoing in the empty space.

"No thanks to you," I mutter. The stranger elbows me in the kidney, eliciting a grunt from me.

"So if you don't mind dear, I'll start to go over the details with Blythe while you use our facilities just out there." She gestures to the main hallway we'd come from.

The woman thanks Marge and rushes into the hallway.

Marge starts up with her venue spiel but I cut her off.

"Actually, Tabitha is known to have..." I pause, as if building to a secret, "issues in the restroom. I really should check on her just in case.

I'll be quick, I promise." I walk as slowly as possible into the hall and lean against the wall next to the restroom door.

This stranger might think she's clever, impersonating my best friend to use luxury facilities, but she's not fooling me. She's not about to sneak out of here and leave me stuck in the middle of a lie. She started this whole charade and she's going to help me finish it.

When the door finally opens, the woman emerges, all worry and urgency gone from her forehead, looking refreshed. Then she walks right past me.

"Where do you think you're going?" I call.

She jumps at the sound, and spins to me, eyes wide. Her hand flies to her chest then when she sees it's me and she lets out a breathy laugh. "You scared the shit out of me! What are you doing over here?"

I stand up straighter and square my shoulders. "Don't be evasive, I asked you first. Where are you going?"

She crosses her arms and raises a brow. It comes across very girl-next-door. "I'm headed back to the ballroom, *Blythe*." She says it slowly and with the hint of a smile on her lips. "Unless you don't want my help. After all, you're a big strong man, I'm sure you've got it covered."

Did I have her pegged wrong? I can usually spot a liar from a mile away, but she seems to be telling the truth. Either way, this is only going to go one way now. "Sweetheart, you're stuck with me for the rest of the day whether you like it or not. You started this charade, and you're sure as hell going to follow through."

"Are you always this charming and trusting?"

"Only towards impulsive redheads."

"We'll just have to work on that then," she says, matter of fact. "For the record, this impulsive redhead goes by Vanessa. So you can use that instead of *sweetheart* in the future, okay, cupcake?"

"Dominic."

She looks me up and down with those round hazel eyes and asks, "Military?"

"Bodyguard."

She makes a show of dramatically looking around, hand to her forehead. "You're sure doing a bang-up job of guarding someone's body right now," she teases.

I scowl. No stranger is this buddy-buddy without an ulterior motive. I just haven't figured out what hers is yet.

She catches me off guard and grabs my hand in hers. "Come on Dominic, let's turn that frown upside-down and be the cutest engaged couple that coordinator has ever seen."

The afternoon is a haze of linen colours and chair styles, cakes sizes and floral arrangements. When I'd agreed to stand-in for Tabby and Blythe, I was hoping I could sign a contract and be done with it. But we're getting an overview of the whole package and everyone here really seems to think Vanessa and I are Tabby and Blythe.

She squeezes my hand.

"Sorry, what was that?" I ask.

"Oh cupcake, you're so spacey today. I asked what colour you're envisioning for our colour scheme. I think the maroon and gold is beautiful."

Tabitha in maroon? Not a chance.

"Tabby, darling, we're having a beach ceremony. Navy and silver are the only acceptable colours, silly." I squeeze her hand back. "It's not like we have to choose right now though. We'll come back to this in a couple weeks when we're more ourselves."

"Of course, you're totally right."

"I know, I'm always right."

"I wouldn't say always—"

Marge's head is pingponging back and forth between us until she can't handle it anymore. "Well, I do believe it's time for supper everyone." She places her hands over our backs and guides us towards the restaurant. "If you approve of everything so far and are impressed by our gourmet chefs — as I'm confident you will be — I'll write up an invoice for your non-refundable deposit and meet you after your meal."

"We can't wait!" Vanessa beams as if this is actually her wedding. She's such a good actress. I'll have to keep an eye on her.

CHAPTER TWO

VANESSA

It's mid-afternoon, so the upscale seafood restaurant is full of empty tables and vacant booths as Dominic and I are seated at a sleek teal and silver booth with cushy bench seats. Dominic gestures for me to sit first and then surprises me by sliding onto the bench next to me. I scrunch my nose in confusion but then it clicks. He's trapped me here. I would have called that clever had there actually been a reason to trap me.

A waiter appears and I grab Dominic's rough hand, putting on the happy couple show until we're left alone with the menus.

I cringe at the drinks list. "That's supposed to be a decimal point, not a comma, right?" I ask, pointing to the prices listed next to the wines.

He wriggles his hand out of mine. "It's all included in our tour today so long as we end up signing a contract for the wedding," he says without tearing his gaze away from the menu.

A muscle works in his jaw, bringing attention to just how sharp and sculpted his tawny face is. My eyes trail lower, wondering if the rest of is six-foot whatever body is just as perfectly toned. He really is a spectacular specimen of the male species. At least as far as appearances go.

"We'd better be convincing enough to get that contract the—"

Dominic turns on me in an instant. "It's time to start talking, *Tabitha*." The words are sharp and full of threat. "Let's start with who the hell you really are and why you're trying to get close to me and my friends."

"I just had to pee," I squeak out. "I promise, that was literally it. I don't know who you are or who Blythe and Tabitha are. My bladder was just super full and you were my shiny golden ticket to the toilets." My hands start to sweat. I knew this guy was paranoid, but he seriously needs to take a vacation day.

Dominic looks me up and down. He's not convinced. "If you were just popping in to take a piss, why are you sticking around? Don't you have somewhere to be?"

"I'm here for…" Hell, I can't focus when those sapphire blue eyes are piercing into my soul. I clear my throat. "Can you please reevaluate your tone? You are getting a free meal with a freaking smoke show at a five star resort." I shake my head. "I'd hate to catch you on a bad day."

I'm not sure if I imagine it, but I could swear he just let out a low growl.

The waiter returns and takes our order, giving me a few seconds to be free of Dominic's gaze. I run a hand through my mane of messy red curls.

As soon as the waiter leaves, I stick out my hand, hoping to take control of this weirdly tense conversation. "Let's try this again!" I try to inject as much cheer into my voice as humanly possible. "My name is Vanessa Ulrich, I'm twenty-eight years old, I've been told I'm a Leo but I honestly know nothing about astrology, and I'm a curatorial assistant at a museum."

I take a chance to rest a hand on his thigh, and damn if it isn't a slab of solid muscle.

He doesn't pull away, but his body stiffens ever so slightly.

Does he still think I'm some sort of threat, or is it something else?

"Don't distract me, you didn't answer my question."

My lip quirks up. "Distract you? I wouldn't dream of it, Dominic, cupcake." I rest my other hand on his thigh too, my confidence growing. I can tell I'm having some sort of effect on him and I'd be lying if I said it didn't charge my body with a thrilling electric hum.

I'm not someone to come onto random men. Hell, I'm not one to go out much. There's just something about the pessimism radiating off this beautiful man that gets under my skin. It's like the universe has presented me with a challenge: crack that rough exterior, elicit a smile, maybe even a laugh. It's hard to imagine, but I want to prove that this man is capable of joy.

He grips me by the wrist then. It's not violent or painful, more of a threat. Then he leans into me and whispers, "Stop playing games, Vanessa Ulrich."

He lets go of me and my hand slips, landing right on a solid erection bulging beneath his pants. Some people have a fight or flight response, but my first instinct is to freeze. I definitely would have been mauled by a sabretooth tiger in the stone ages.

Heat floods my face and my brain suddenly forgets how to brain. "I drove up here for Annihilation Royalle, but it doesn't start until tomorrow so I have some time to kill. I didn't mean to butt into your life, but...toilets. And now food."

Right on cue the waiter returns with our plates and the savoury smell of my Alaskan halibut brings me back to my senses. I remove myself from Dominic's lap, to his visible relief, and thank the waiter who graciously doesn't comment on seeing me groping my fake fiancée.

We eat in silence after that. Just the sounds of forks scraping and ice clinking in Dominic's water glass. He has the chance to try hundred dollar wines and he chooses water. It must be a paranoid bodyguard thing. Thankfully I'm not a bodyguard. I take a sip of my Cabernet Sauvignon and it tastes like... wine. How anticlimactic.

Just as we're finishing up, my stomach loudly announces that it's digesting my food. I give a sheepish smile and look at Dominic.

He rolls his eyes, biting into his last piece of steak.

"I really don't belong in a fancy restaurant, in case you couldn't tell," I say as way of apology.

"What is Annihilation Royalle?" he abruptly asks.

My eyes light up and I dive into an explanation of the MMO RPG game that fully takes place in the ocean, under water. "You can be a scuba diving human, a shark person, a mermaid, an octo-person — it's really fucking cool. There's a battle royalle tournament for it just a couple blocks away at this cool retro game bar. It's nothing big, but it's my favourite game and it was originally created in my hometown. So..." I shrug. "I practically have to show up. Not that it's a chore, I literally cannot wait."

"Figuratively," Dominic says.

"What?"

"You figuratively cannot wait. If you literally could not wait, you would be there right now, not waiting here."

I muse that over as I take the last bite of my fish, then abruptly stand up on the bench seat. The bartender across the room scrunches his brow and looks around, not sure if he should do something about the crazy girl standing on the restaurant furniture.

"You're right. I need to go!" I take a theatrically large step over Dominic who swiftly snatches me up by the waist as if I'm feather-light and brings me to sit on his lap.

My eyes widen and I let out a surprised giggle, both at how swiftly he managed the act and how intimate it is with his arm wrapped around my stomach.

Then he softly brushes my ear with his lips. "You're not going anywhere, dear fiancée. Now you'd best behave yourself so we don't prematurely ruin a wedding."

Is that a smile I feel on his lips?

I open my mouth to respond, but on my inhale, air gets mixed with a piece of fish. I try to gasp for oxygen but the fish lodges in my airway and all that escapes are choking coughs.

Dominic calmly slides us out of the booth, bends me over his muscled arm, and delivers jarring back blows. The fifth time his palm lands between my shoulder blades, the piece of fish dislodges and goes skittering across the marble floor.

I continue to cough, trying to dispel that gross scratchy feeling from my throat as Dominic guides me back to the booth to sit down, rubbing circles on my back. The warmth of his palm and the gesture itself is so kind and reassuring. I don't want him to stop touching me.

"Are you okay miss?" The waiter reappears in a buzz of energy, asking me a million questions about my wellbeing, offering me water, the whole production. Dominic tries to wave him off, but the waiter doesn't leave until he's issued us a free couples massage as an apology for the poor dining experience.

"Thank you," I rasp when I can finally speak again.

"For the basic human decency of saving your life? Don't mention it."

The list of things I know about Dominic includes: he's a body-guard, he's super paranoid, he's not a vegetarian, he is the picture of chiselled beauty, and he can't take a compliment.

"Don't be stubborn, just accept my thanks," I urge. It strikes me as being really important that Dominic accepts my gratitude. Everyone needs to accept kindness and praise where it's due. I can't imagine going through life with a glass half empty like him.

He just grunts.

We'll work on that.

CHAPTER THREE

DOMINIC

I flick the pen across the bottom of the contract, creating my own version of Blythe's signature. It looks more like an accidental scratch when compared to Vanessa's bubbly script next to it.

"Right, thank you, Marge," I announce, getting up to leave. "It's been a pleasure, but we best be going."

Vanessa stands too, grabbing my hand. My fingers interlock with hers as if on instinct. I'm surprised at how weirdly normal the gesture feels already. It's just acting, I tell myself. I'm just really committed to selling us as a couple.

Marge thanks us for our business and stands, holding out her hand to us.

I go to shake it only to realize that she's not holding out her hand, she's holding out a room card. "We have you in the honeymoon suite on the eighteenth floor," she announces. "The same one you'll be in the night of your wedding. If there are any changes you'd like made to it for your special day, please just let a staff member know."

Marge's mouth is still moving but my mind isn't comprehending a thing she's saying. I'm too focused on Vanessa's mouth that's drawn into a little 'o' of surprise.

I'm such an idiot. Tabby had told me about the accommodations I'd have here, but I've been distracted. Vanessa was this unexpected curveball that's smacked me right upside the head, giving me a concussion, driving rational thought from my brain.

I take the room card from Marge, thank her, and guide Vanessa to the empty elevator. It isn't until the door's shut and we're alone that I finally turn to Vanessa. "I have to say that I appreciated your help today. So it's only fair I repay the favour. There's an emergency exit, in the ballroom — not hooked up to any alarm that I could see. We'll give Marge a few minutes to vacate the room, then I'll help you sneak out."

Vanessa puts her hands on her hips and cocks her head. "What the hell are you talking about?"

I scoff and run a hand through my black hair. It doesn't escape my notice when her eyes dart to my beltline as my shirt peaks up.

"I'm talking about getting you out of here without blowing our cover. If the staff see you leave with all your stuff," I gesture to her backpack, "they'll know we're not a couple. And we obviously can't share a room."

She steps closer to me with a devious glint in her eye and wraps her arms around mine, like she did when we'd first met. "Obviously? You sure know how to hurt a girl's feelings," she teases.

The elevator dings and the doors slide open.

"Let's at least see the room first," she says, heading down the hall. "Look at this place! Chances are it'll be so big we won't even have to breathe the same air tonight. Which is perfect because I don't want your pessimism to rub off on me anyway."

Fuck. Blood rushes to my dick at the thought of rubbing off on Vanessa. Her on her knees in the hotel room, her pretty pink mouth smiling up at me as my seed explodes over the constellation of freckles on her cheeks and her sleek red curls.

"Dominic, the card please!" She makes a grabby gesture and I hand her the key card, trying to shake off whatever the fuck my mind just conjured. I do not fuck humans. That might be okay for Tabby, but I'm perfectly happy visiting the Passions Bay Pod caverns for a good fuck from many-limbed cecaelia every week. The idea of mixing with another species is just too weird. It's not for me. It's not—

Vanessa swings the door open and gawks at the luxury suite. "This is amazing!"

I follow after her and have to admit, she's right. Over the past year I'd gotten used to living in Walton Manor with its rustic grandeur and extravagance, but this place is completely different with its modern charm. Floor to ceiling windows give us a view of the starry sky over the ocean and when I flick on the light, a crystal chandelier sparkles from the ridiculously high ceilings. A plush king bed sits in the middle of the room and a deep soaker tub sits just off to the side, completely exposed. One thing I've come to realize about human habitation is that if furniture is in the middle of a space instead of against a wall, it's luxury. But this is more than just luxury, it's...*romantic*. Yikes.

Everything in this room is big enough to fit me in my cecaelia form *and* Vanessa.

No, I'm not going there.

"Welcome to the king suite!" a man announces, stepping out of the bathroom.

I instinctively wrap my arm across Vanessa's chest and pull her to me, shielding her from the stranger in the room. But then I get a good look at him with his hotel uniform. He's carrying robes and is headed for a massage table I didn't notice.

Right, the free massage. I didn't realize it would be right now.

I quickly release Vanessa whose lips are pressed together in an obviously poor attempt at hiding her amusement. I fully realize she thinks I'm an overprotective asshole, and maybe she's right. But I'd rather be careful than dead.

The masseuse welcomes us and hands us skimpy silk robes and slippers.

Vanessa pulls her shoulders back, releasing a loud crack and sighs. "I am so looking forward to this."

Once we're robed up Vanessa enthusiastically hops up on the table and lays facedown. I pretend to be looking out the window to avoid seeing her disrobe, but I still catch her reflection in the glass. The masseuse folds down the silky white robe at the dip of her lower back so that it's draped over the curve of her ass.

In cecaelia society, nudity is the norm. But there's something about seeing the soft curvature of Vanessa that has heat rushing to my face. And other places.

"Let's begin!" The masseuse claps his hands together. "This way please, Mr. Blythe."

"I'm sorry?" I turn and see him gesturing to Vanessa's side.

"Don't be shy, I'll show you how to have magic hands like me." He holds up his palms and wiggles his fingers.

You can't be fucking serious.

The next thing I know, my fingers are in her soft curls, gently applying pressure in circular motions under the direction of our instructor. This close, I can smell her coconut shampoo. One of my favourite smells.

It isn't until I make it down to her naked back, kneading her tense muscles, that Vanessa really gets into it. I press at a spot just below her shoulder blade, feeling a tight knot come apart beneath my hands. She lets out a series of soft moans as I work her and those sounds alone wreak havoc on my body. I want to hear it again, so I move to her other side and repeat the motion. The vibrations of her moan radiate through my hands and more blood rushes to by cock which is rock hard by now. The fact that I can cause a human to make those sounds with just my hands on their back... this is new territory for me.

Much too soon, Vanessa's turn on the table is over. She looks adorably sleepy and content with her heavy lids and soft smile, hair mused from my hands in it. Then before I know it, she's on her tip toes and I tilt my head down to meet her lips. It's not an electric kiss or even a teasing one like I would have expected from her. It's gentle and lazy and feels like the most natural thing.

"Ok my lovelies, let's leave the canoodling until I've left the room, yes?" the masseuse says with a cheeky tone.

Vanessa bites her lip, staving off a laugh at my horrified expression. I'd nearly forgotten he was in the room, that this was just an act for him. I turn away from Vanessa — this siren who's messing with my head — and get on the table facedown, subtly readjusting myself so my erection doesn't punch a hole through the table. As a cecaelia with the gift of extreme strength, I wouldn't put it past the realm of possibility. *Good luck explaining that one to these humans*, I think.

The minute Vanessa's hands are on my head and neck, hot tingles shoot through my skin like fireworks in my dermis. After a while my mind tunes out the masseuse's instructions and all I can focus on are the millions of sensations taking over my body.

"You're so tense," Vanessa whispers as she works my back. "Shock-er."

I roll my eyes even though I can feel the stress melting away under the pressure of Vanessa's hands and the way she works her fingers.

I hear a click and look up then. "What was that?"

"That's the sound of privacy at last," she whispers, wrapping her hands around my bicep.

A sigh escapes my lips. Maybe I should be getting massages more often because I don't recall having ever felt this light. It's like Vanessa's a cecaelia with the gift of soothing.

I shoot upright and stare at her.

"Woah and here I thought you were finally learning to relax. I promise I wasn't about to assassinate you in your vulnerable state mister bodyguard."

I shake my head. "Did you just use a gift on me?"

She blinks. "I wouldn't call my massage skills a gift per-se but thank you. I think that's the closest to giving me a compliment you've come today. I'd say we're making progress."

Okay, not a cecaelia then.

My shoulders relax. If I had gone this long, oblivious to a cecaelia in my presence, I'd have to retire as a bodyguard. I'd never live down that shame. But she's just an insignificant little human.

"Sweetheart, I'm not a pet project for you to solve. And I think it's time for you to go." I hop off the table, my robe falling to the floor and I'm completely naked before her. Even though nakedness is the norm where I'm from, I'm also aware that it's taboo for humans and hope this gesture scares Vanessa off once and for all.

She looks me up and down, the jump of her eyebrows barely imperceptible as she takes me all in before meeting my eyes again.

"You want to know what I think, cupcake? I think you've done a terrible job of hiding that boner all day. I think you like to push people away because of a misguided sense of self-preservation. I also think I'm going to stay here tonight." With that she raises both hands and flops back onto the giant bed that swallows her hole, her hair bouncing out around her in a red halo. "It sure beats the motel I'd be at otherwise."

I cross my arms at the foot of the bed but I'm drawn to that infectious smile. Then I see the way her nipples are peaked and hard under the thin fabric of her robe.

Fuck it, she's not wrong about me.

"I think you're too optimistic for your own good," I say.

She props herself up on her elbows to look at me and counters, "I think you're too grouchy. We sure make quite the engaged couple."

I make a split second decision right then and kneel between Vanessa's legs that are dangling off the bed. "Contrary to your profile of me, I do know how to relax."

Her breath hitches as she gazes down at me, poised at her feet. But she quickly regains her composure and chooses her words carefully.

"You can do whatever you want, cupcake, as long as it makes you happy."

Chapter Four

VANESSA

Dominic lets out a low feral growl that has my hands twitching for him. Without hesitation, his strong hands wrap around my love handles and he pulls me to him. He picks me up like I weigh nothing and throws me over his shoulder.

I let out a yelp and am about to protest when Dominic gently lays me on the massage table so that my ass is right on the edge of the surface. Then he kneels in front of me.

My breath hitches and my pulse is in a league of its own at the rate it's pounding.

With one tug on the string, he undoes my robe, the silk sliding off around me, baring me to him like a gift.

"This will only work if you promise to tell me when to stop," he says, surprising me with his seriousness.

"Of course," I say.

And just like that his muscles relax and a smile plays at his lips.

"Listen carefully, sweetheart. You told me to do whatever makes me happy and I intend to do just that. What I need from you is obedience. Do you think you can do that for me?"

His warm breath on my thighs sends goosebumps erupting over my body and he notices too because he lets out a low chuckle.

"Yes, I can obey you," I breathe. What else could I possibly say to this gorgeous man between my legs right now?

"Good," he rasps. "Now I want you to keep your eyes on me the entire time. I want you to see me feast on your cunt and I want you to watch yourself get devoured."

The mouth on this man has me blushing a highlighter shade of red — if he's hungry for a literal strawberry, I guess he's in luck.

I nod, gazing into his stormy ocean blue eyes and he stares right back as he drapes my legs over his shoulders and dips his head down.

Heat erupts from my core as Dominic's hot mouth meets my pussy. His hums of satisfaction against my sensitive flesh has me wanting to close my eyes and give into the bliss but I hold his gaze as instructed.

With a flick of his tongue against my clit, Dominic has me bucking on the table. Then he pulls away, clicking his tongue. "I thought I told you to watch me, Vanessa. If you can't listen, you'll have to be punished." His eyes flash with something that has my body thrumming.

Again, he picks me up like I'm feather-light and places me on the other end of the table so I'm straddling the open hole in the headrest.

"What are you doing?" I breathe.

"Teaching you a lesson."

He presses a button which makes the table slowly rise, until I'm at the perfect height for him to—

I gasp as Dominic plunges into me through the hole in the headrest.

"Eyes on me now, sweetheart," he orders.

I do as commanded and meet his gaze. His lip quirks with smug satisfaction as he pulls out and plunges into me again. I brace my hands on his abs for balance and feel the hard flex of his muscles as he moves inside me.

But it's not enough. The headrest is in the way of me fully taking him in.

I let out a whimper.

"Tell me what you want, Vanessa." He stops abruptly, dick poised at my entrance, teasing me.

"I want you to fuck me with your massive cock — with the whole thing," I say without hesitation.

"Can such a small thing handle all that cock?" He steps back so I have an unobstructed view of him. Domonic fully erect and radiating lust is a vision. But his question wasn't a cocky exaggeration. His dick really is bigger than any I've ever taken before. Hell, I don't know how it would physically fit inside me.

A bead of precum glistens on his tip.

I hesitate and then settle on a tentative solution.

"Maybe I'll take it somewhere else instead this time," I suggest. And because it sounds like fun to disrupt his power trip, I rearrange myself so I'm laying facedown on the table like I was during my massage. "I'm ready," I call.

A few beats later, a pulsing cock obstructs my view of the floor. I'm ready for it though. I open my mouth and Dominic's salty tang fills my senses as he slowly thrusts into my mouth.

At first, I completely second guess this plan. But on his second thrust, I relax my muscles and fully take him into me. The muscles in my throat expand to accommodate his bulk until his balls hit the bottom of the headrest.

"What a good girl you are to take me in like that," he praises. "Do you like my big cock filling your pretty mouth?"

He pulls out and I pant, "I fucking love your big cock inside me." And I do. If I can take this monster cock, what else am I capable of?

This time when Dominic thrusts into my mouth, he leans over me and his fingers plunge into my pussy with a wet squelch. I'm so wet for this man and feel myself instantly clench around his fingers.

He lets out a deep growl and I feel a pang of satisfaction knowing that I can elicit that reaction from such a guarded person.

We set into a rhythm of his cock in my throat and fingers in my pussy and it doesn't take long before I can't take it anymore and explode around his fingers. The sensation sends him following me over the edge as he plunges deep into me and hot cum fills my throat.

"Don't forget this." Dominic tosses my satchel to me as I exit the restroom. I somehow catch it with one hand, making it look effortless, then promptly toss it onto the bench, continuing to wring my wet hair into a towel.

"I already told you, I'm not going anywhere. I earned a night here just as much as you did and there's nothing you can do about it."

I cross the room and draw the massive curtains shut. I really hope these windows are only one way, or else... I look at the beach below. Surely nobody would've been out this late.

"If money's an issue, I can pay for your new room in some other hotel. But you can't stay here, sweetheart."

"Sure I can!" I crawl under the fluffy white comforter and sink into the bed, my exhausted body melting into the plush heaven. My matching white pajama set is so cozy against my skin, there's no way I'm leaving. I let out a huge yawn. In any case, Domonic has thoroughly warn me out. I'm not going anywhere.

I eye Dom, scowling at the end of the bed in his black v-neck and grey boxer shorts. It's not that I expected him to put on the hotel pjs, but their thread count surely would have cheered him up a little. Was I a little bummed that he reverted right back to the grumpy asshole after sex? Honestly, a little. But I'm trying not to take it personally. "And money isn't the issue — well not completely. I just don't understand why you're so but-hurt over this. This bed is so big, you won't even know I'm here."

A muscle works in his jaw. I really don't know what the big deal is. Surely he knows by now that I'm not some crazy assassin sent to infiltrate his little friend group. Right?

Without another word, he grabs an extra duvet from a linen closet, shakes it out, and tosses it in the deep soaker tub along with a few pillows from the bed.

"Dominic please, don't be ridiculous. This bed is plenty big enough for the both of us and your giant schlong." He doesn't so much as crack a smile, let alone acknowledge I'd spoken at all.

And that's how I had mind blowing sex with a stranger at a fancy hotel and regretted it after.

CHAPTER FIVE

VANESSA

I look at my phone with groggy eyes, squinting past the onslaught of backlight. It's four in the morning and Dominic is making a racket in the tub like he keeps elbowing the ceramic.

"Dude, keep it down!" I whisper shout and toss one of the extra pillows at him. The muffled thud tells me it's a direct hit to the head.

He's quiet for a couple minutes and I'm about to fall asleep again when a couple more bangs echo. I roll out of bed and walk over to the tub with my eyes half closed.

The thudding continues at odd intervals and it's not until I'm knelt down and peering over the edge of the tub that I realize he must be having a nightmare. The duvet is gripped in his hands like a lifeline and he's twitching all over the place like he's locked in battle.

I hesitate for a minute, not sure if I should wake him up or if this is like a sleepwalker situation where you're supposed to let them sleep and just ensure their safety. What if some bodyguard reflex kicks in and he lashes out at me? His head violently twitches to the side, bonking off the tub with a loud thud.

I grab him by his shoulder and shake. "Dominic, it's just a dream, tough guy. Come on back to the land of the living now." He doesn't stir. The thrashing stops. I wait a few seconds to make sure he doesn't start up again, but when I remove my hand from his shoulder, he's back in fight mode.

"Dominic!" I shout. But again he doesn't hear me and keeps on fighting, so I grab his bicep to shake him again.

Wow that's a solid bicep.

The minute I make contact with his skin, he relaxes again, muscles going slack, breathing slowed. I brush a lock of soft hair out of his face. His jaw slackens and his lips half part, making him look so peaceful.

What do I do now? I can't sit here all night to scare away his bad dreams. I don't see any other option so I retrieve the duvet and some pillows from the bed as quickly as I can and return my hand to Dom's arm. I push the sheets and pillows around, trying to make a nest that'll allow me to sleep sitting up like this, half in the tub, but it's useless.

I puff out a breath. I have an idea but even thinking it sounds weird and invasive. On the other hand, Dominic had fucked me through the face hole of a massage table less than twelve hours ago, so where even is the line? If I want any sleep tonight I don't really have any other options, so I crawl into the tub with Dominic.

I'm half hoping my weight on top of him will be enough to wake him up, but instead a muscled arm wraps around my waist and pulls me against the solid wall of his chest. We're spooning. I knew he was a big softie, even if he can only show it while unconscious. But the important thing is that his thrashing has stopped, his heartbeat against my back has returned to a normal rhythm and his breathing is coming easy again.

I blink away the sunlight streaming into the room through the sheer curtains. Hadn't I just closed my eyes to sleep? It takes me a minute to remember where I am. I go to rub the sleep from my eyes but find my arms don't move.

"What the—"

I look down to see thick velvety tendrils of warm muscle wrapped around my body like a gothic cocoon.

I wiggle and arm free and tentatively brush my fingers along a tendril. The substance immediately constricts at my touch, trapping my hand against my body. It doesn't hurt but the sudden movement elicits a yelp of surprise from me.

Dominic stirs against my back. "What's wrong? Are you okay?"

With my head under his chin, I feel the moment his pulse goes into overdrive and he pulls away from me.

Suddenly those constricting tendrils are gone and a wave of cool hotel room air washes over me as I spin on my big spoon. Dom is already halfway across the room with—

I must still be dreaming because Dominic looks exactly like one of those octo-people from Annihilation Royalle. He's the kind of solid lean human muscle from the waist up that you only see in movies or online. His boxers lay in tatters on the floor having been shredded to bits by his tentacles. That's right, freaking tentacles. Just below his abs, his skin morphs into a deep blue and splits off into eight thick appendages half covered in undulating suckers.

Definitely a dream.

"Can I touch them," I ask, already getting out of the tub.

"Fuck," he says through clenched teeth, "this is what I was afraid of."

When I get a few paces closer, Dominic shakes his head and suddenly his tentacles retract into him and legs sprout from his torso like the CGI you'd see on a CW show.

"Sorry, I didn't meet to make you feel uncomfortable. I was just curious."

He quickly throws on a pair of jeans and then he's right in front of me. "You're not responding logically, Vanessa. What aren't you telling me?"

He is so damn sexy towering over me, trying to stamp down the adrenaline I can still feel radiating off him as excess heat.

I put my hand on my hips. "I thought we were past the suspicion phase! Please don't ruin this for me, I've never seen an octo-person before. Can you please just..." I spread my hands like I'm smoothing down a dress to gesture him shifting back into his octo-person form. "Please?" I widen my eyes and stick out my bottom lip.

His cock jumps against my thigh through his jeans and I raise a brow.

"*He* doesn't seem suspicious of me."

"Gods damn, Vanessa," he growls. Then his hand cups the back of my head and he spins, pressing me into the wall with his body.

I gasp in delight as his mouth meets mine in a desperate, frustrated kiss. Then he leans his forehead against mine and lets out a sigh. "I don't understand. I had you trapped in a tentacle cocoon and you're not even remotely freaked out by any of this, are you?"

"I've had weirder tentacle dreams," I say, biting my lip. "Playing a game with octo-people for years will do that to a woman."

He tilts my chin up and looks me directly in the eyes. "Vanessa, you are not dreaming." He says it so seriously, all frustrated lust gone from his voice.

Of course I'm dreaming and of course my dreams would escalate to trying to convince me this is real.

"Ouch!" I flinch away from where he just pinched my arm. *Way to kill the mood.*

Then Dominic's frame shoots up like he's having a freak growth spurt. His tentacles are back.

I pinch my own bicep this time and freeze.

"Ah there it is," Dominic almost sounds relieved. "Don't worry little human, I'll make it so it's like this never even happened."

While I stand immobile against the wall, he slips his phone out of his pocket and dials a number, talking in hushed tones as he paces the room. When he hangs up, he smiles. "You're on house arrest for the rest of the day — until my mage can get here to wipe your memory of this." He gestures to his writhing limbs.

"Wait, I can't be stuck here. I have a tournament to get to!" Just like that, the spell is broken and I have control of my body again. "Shit, what time is it?" The sun is well in the sky and the tournament starts just after noon. I go to grab my phone but a tentacle shoots out and grips me around the wrist, stopping my progress. It doesn't hurt, rather the suckers wrapped around me almost tickle my delicate flesh. So fascinating. "Dominic, this is important. Let me go now."

He effortlessly lifts me off the ground and sets me in the bathtub. He doesn't remove his tentacles though. I tug at them and flinch when I accidentally finger a sucker. "I've been looking forward to this all year, and I promise I won't tell anyone about you. I'll even come back here after so you can wipe my memory Men in Black style."

"Sorry sweetheart," he says, leaning against the wall beside the tub. "Can't take any chances."

I try a different approach. He seems like an analytical guy, maybe if I can appeal to reason... "I'm expected there today, you know. I'm ranked number one in the world right now. Someone will notice me missing and get worried when I don't answer my phone."

Dominic shrugs. He just shrugs!

So I shrug too and sit in the blanket nest of a bathtub. "That's okay, we can just hangout here and sing ABBA."

He raises a brow at that. "You do not listen to ABBA."

"No, but my roommate did. Incessantly. You could say I learned all the words to every song against my will. And now you can too!" If he won't listen to reason, maybe I can annoy him into compliance.

I don't give him a chance to protest before grabbing the mini bottle of eucalyptus conditioner as my microphone and begin an extra loud, off-key rendition of Dancing Queen. Dominic's grip on me loosens as he covers his ears with his hands. I take the opportunity to hop onto the bed and continue my performance from there.

"Feel the beat from the tambourine, oh yeaaaaah!"

"Vanessa, cut it out."

"You can dance—"

"Vanessa!"

"You can jive—"

Quick as a whip, two tentacles shoot out, one wrapping around my waist and the other covering my mouth. Dominic really resembles the octo-people from Annihilation Royalle and somehow that brings me comfort. As if I know him. I wonder if he has the same weakness as the octo-people from the game...

I continue singing, the muffled notes vibrating through his suckers over my mouth.

Just as I'd hoped, Dominic pulls back his appendage, rubbing it with his hand.

"Ticklish?" I ask with a wink. I take my moment of freedom to stride over to my backpack for a change of clothes.

"How could you possibly know that?" he asks. I can see the wheels spinning in his head, trying to figure out when he could have let that information slip yesterday.

I slip off my pajamas and hear the tiniest intake of breath behind me. I smile to myself as I slip on a black racerback crop top and high-waisted wide leg cargo pants. Then I position my headphones around my neck and turn to him. Dominic's taken a seat on the lounger and is trying to subtly readjust the front of his pants.

"It's from Annihilation Royalle. As an octo-person, how do you not know about the most popular game with octo-people? That would be like me not knowing Sophie Turner or Madeline Petsch. Hashtag redheads unite!"

Dominic's brow furrows. "I don't know who those people are, but my people are called cecaelia, not octo-people." He finally works out a comfortable sitting position for his boner and continues. "So what else has your little game told you about my kind?"

An idea strikes then.

I stuff my phone charger and pajamas into my backpack and sling it over my shoulder. "Guess you'll just have to escort me to the tournament and find out!" I flash him a brilliant smile.

He opens his mouth to respond but I cut him off. "Don't worry, you can wipe my brain or whatever after, Agent D."

CHAPTER SIX

DOMINIC

My driver pulls up to a café decked out in neon lights that look uninspired in the bright afternoon light. Dozens of twenty and thirty year olds of varying bold aesthetics filter into the venue.

Vanessa and I are about to leave the backseat when a vibrating sensation makes us both jump.

"Oh shit!" she says, pulling her phone out and scrolling to a remote controlled egg vibrator app, hitting the off button. The vibrations in her backpack stop.

"Now I need to know why you have that at a video game tournament," I say, angling myself towards her.

She bites her lip, debating whether or not to spill, before letting out a sigh. "Okay but you cannot tell anyone. I know you don't know anyone in the gaming community, but I mean it. Nobody."

I motion zipping up my lips.

"I wear an egg vibrator when I play sometimes," she confesses. "It just gets my adrenaline going and I perform nine percent better with it. Call it a trade secret."

I pull out my own phone and download the app.

"What are you doing?" she asks, trying to get a good look at my phone screen.

I hand it to her. "Sync it up with your vibrator."

To my surprise she doesn't argue or come back with any smart ass comments. She just connects my phone to her vibrator.

Holy hell, it's getting really hot in here.

When she hands my phone back, her pupils are dilated and her fingers brush mine. "I have thirty minutes before the first round starts," she whispers.

At those words I close the privacy screen between us and the driver. Vanessa raises a brow at me suggestively and that little action breaks me. My hands wrap around her sides and I pull her onto my lap so that she's straddling me. Her eyes are wide with surprise, just as they were when I threw her around last night. *Fuck*, last night.

She fumbles for the button on my jeans but I push her hands away. "Oh no my greedy little gamer girl, I intend to have more fun with this."

I reach into her bag and pull out the little pink egg vibrator.

Her lips part as realization dawns.

"Now I want you to be a good girl and win this tournament with me in control the whole time. Can you do that for me?"

Her thighs squeeze my legs and by cock hardens at attention, tenting under her hovering center. "You'll need to reward me after," she says.

"Of course, sweetheart. You will always be rewarded for being a good little slut." Then I slide down her pants just enough for me to gain access with the toy. My fingers play across her folds that are already so wet that the device slides right in.

By the time we're in the venue, lanyard badges around our necks, we've both made ourselves presentable. I watch Vanessa greeting other gamers and autographing posters with genuine enthusiasm and excitement. I don't think I fully believed her when she told me she was ranked number one for this game, but it's clear that she's a celebrity here. Even though I don't really know her, I still feel a pang of pride.

Nobody could ever guess that this bubbly redhead wears a vibrator in public as part of her strategic plan. Hell, I know about it and I still have a hard time believing it.

So I decide to give myself a reminder. I discretely pull out my phone and press the pulsating button at the same moment Vanessa's scrawling her name on someone's poster. The second it kicks in, she jumps, her marker making a scrawl across the page. She blinks away her momentary surprise and turns that scribble into a giant heart. Composed again, Vanessa graciously thanks her fan for coming today.

She scowls at me and I wink in return. This is going to be fun.

Vanessa is truly amazing at what she does. Having never indulged in videogames myself, I thought it was going to be easy. That is until I said so to Vanessa.

"Here, join the casual players over here and give it a shot!" she says, seating me in a gaming chair and putting giant headphones on me. After designing my character: a cecae — no, octo-person — wielding a rocket launcher with a battle axe strapped to its back, the round begins. My avatar is air-dropped into the battle royalle map along with the dozens of other players. We plunge into a vividly teal ocean at the same time, at which point I get a look at the arena for the first time. Kelp forests, ship wrecks, castles that look like they're straight out of a kids mermaid movie. No cecaelia caverns though, I note.

I quickly realize I have no clue how to control my avatar. I examine the keyboard and start jamming the arrow keys.

My character doesn't move.

I jab my finger over and over again into the forward arrow but nothing happens. Suddenly I take hold of the mouse and now I'm spinning in circles, looking at the sky. What in the fresh robotics are these controls?

Then a shark-man with a tiny dagger swims up behind my character from out of nowhere and stabs him right in the shoulder. It's fatal. I can tell by the slow-mo replay. My character sinks to the sandy ground and that's that. The other player celebrates by repeatedly crouching his avatar over my avatar's face. Real mature.

Vanessa removes my headphones and gives me a consolatory pat on the shoulder. "Damn you really bombed that. At least you're good at other things!" She says it with a wink, to which I respond by intensifying the vibrator.

Her eyes go wide and she visibly swallows. "Well played."

Over the course of three hours, Vanessa has managed to climb all the way to the championship round. Her avatar is a tiny human named Valkyrie Deathshroud who sports an orange scuba diving suit decked out with obnoxious orange bunny ears and dominates every arena with her exploding harpoon.

Now in the final round, Vanessa's sitting in the circle of computers with five others, her orange bunny ear headphones making her easy to spot from across the café. I can't explain why bunny Vanessa is so sexy, but I definitely want us to whip out those headphones sometime when we're alone.

What am I saying? I'm going to have her memory wiped soon and then she won't remember me at all. I need to get it together. Everything will be back to normal in a few hours.

"Dominic, I need your help!" Vanessa calls from her station.

Like the dutiful assistant I've realized I'd become at this event, I head over and crouch beside her chair. "Yes, sweetheart?"

She looks me straight in the eyes. "For this final round, I need you to sync that app to the game audio."

She brings up a sync code on the computer and I connect the app without question. My kinky girl is going full immersion with this final round. I head back to my stool at the coffee bar and watch as the final round of the evening begins.

One by one the competition dwindles until it's only Vanessa and a pink-haired woman in cat ear headphones left. At this point, the playing arena has shrunk so much that there's no hiding from each other. I watch, transfixed as Vanessa's fingers fly across the keyboard, hunting down the competition. Five minutes later it's all over. Vanessa's humanoid bunny leaps up straight in the water, harpoon held in front of her and pierces the enemy from foot to head like a macabre kabob.

I jump up along with the rest of the audience in a cacophony of cheers — and boos from the opposing fans. After the host of the tournament declares Vanessa the winner and awards her with her cash prize, she spends the next half hour taking pictures with fans and other players. Though I note how she keeps catching my eye. I hadn't let up on her torturous pleasure just because she'd won and I can tell it's getting to her. So I get in line for a photo with her and when it's my turn, I whisk her up in my arms.

She lets out a happy yelp of surprise and subsequently has to placate the security guard, letting him know she's fine. That I'm fine.

I kick open the front door to where my driver's waiting at the curb, toss our bags into the back seat, and then follow them in ourselves.

As soon as the door is closed behind us, Vanessa's straddling me, her mouth soft and desperate on mine.

"I want you to shift," she pants, pulling away.

I shake my head, running my hands up and down the curves of her body. "There isn't enough room in here and I want to reward you properly. You were fucking amazing out there and I intend to fuck you like the insanely talented and sexy winner you are."

Chapter Seven

VANESSA

"Then take me somewhere else and fuck me like a winner," I say.

Between the excitement and adrenaline of winning the tournament, learning cecaelia are a thing, and being accompanied by a cecaelia male who's in control of my pleasure device in public, I need release. I need Dominic to do everything he just promised and more.

We don't manage to keep our hands to ourselves on the drive back to the hotel, but I'm able to control myself long enough for me and Dominic to make it back to our suite. The minute the door clicks closed behind us, tentacles erupt from the man before me, sending tattered shreds of black jean flying in every direction.

I'm still half convinced I'm dreaming because who could have asked for a better winner's celebration than being ravished in a luxury hotel room by a real honest to god, hot-ass cecaelia man? I may have had a dream along these lines a couple times after some particularly long Annihilation Royalle streams.

"What do those tentacles do?" I ask, stepping closer and reaching out to touch them. They're not slimy like one might think. It weirdly reminds me of the feel of my brother's ball python — solid muscle, smooth, and firm. But unlike a snake, Dominic's tentacles are softer, more velvety.

I wrap my hand around the one tentacle and feel his suckers affix to my palm. He shutters so I must be doing something right.

His phone rings then, pulling us both out of the moment. He definitely isn't human because who doesn't have their phone set to vibrate at all times?

He looks at the caller ID and back to me all apologetic. "I need to take this, but I'll be right back."

I nod, trying to stamp down my disappointment. Then I catch a glimpse of his phone as he turns to the bathroom for some privacy. It's Tabitha calling.

I drop onto the bench, fanning myself. It totally makes sense that he'd stop everything to answer a call from Tabitha. She's the whole reason he's here. Besides, it's probably in his job description that he needs to always be available to her in case she's in trouble or something.

"Tabby, is everything all right?"

I creep closer to the bathroom door. Is it really eavesdropping if Dominic is just speaking too loudly in my vicinity? Call me curious. Does Tabitha know what Dominic is? Is she a cecaelia too?

"That's right. The papers are all signed and you guys officially have a venue for a killer wedding." After a pause: "Sorry I'm not back yet. I'm waiting on the mage to get here. There's been a bit of an... issue. Nothing a quick memory wipe can't fix though. He should get here soon, I'm just killing time with the human." Another pause. "Oh fuck off, it's not like that. I'm not a human-lover like you, nor do I ever intend to be one. Blythe is nice enough but I maintain they're horrible."

Just like that my heart drops to the floor, staining the plush white carpet a heartbreak red. If I thought Dominic was really coming around to liking me, I was sorely mistaken. Yes, he'd told me about the memory wipe and yes, I knew he was leaving town today, but for a second there I was having so much fun with him. My stupid heart let the idea slip that maybe something could come of us. But no. He's just killing time with a stupid human before he can get rid of her.

I look at my watch but realize I don't know what time the mage is supposed to get here. The room feels like its closing in on me. I have to get out of here. I swing my backpack over my shoulder and head straight out the door. The hallway is deserted as I start jabbing my finger at the elevator call button. For such a luxury place with so many floors, you'd think they'd have more elevators. My finger doesn't stop until the doors slide open and I walk right into a man in my haste to get out of here.

"Shit, I'm so sorry—" I start and stop short. The man is wearing an orange hoodie, green plaid kilt, and mismatched shoes. One white runner and one dirty yellow flipflop. The senile old man look makes me wonder how he made it past reception on his own. Then it clicks.

"You're the mage," I say, already knowing the words are true. No magicless human being would be able to look like this in such an upscale establishment.

His grey eyes examine me up and down and I get the sense he's gleaming more than just my physical appearance.

"Hello Vanessa," he says, his words soft and soothing, completely contradicting his unhinged appearance. "May I ask where Dominic is?"

I wave off his question, gesturing for us both to get in the elevator. Once the doors close, I swipe my arm over all the buttons for all the floors, and they light up like an inconvenient Christmas tree. "So I hear you have this magical mind wiping ability?"

He nods, hands folded in front of him.

"I've had quite the day and would appreciate if you did it as soon as possible. Now would be amazing. You can tell Dominic about it later. Is that okay?" I wrap my arms around myself. "It won't hurt, right?"

The old man takes my hand in both of his in a reassuring gesture. "It shan't hurt a bit," he says and instructs me to sit cross legged on the floor while he sits in front of me. The whole time I'm just hoping nobody gets on the elevator with us as the doors ping open every twenty seconds at each new floor on our way down to the lobby.

The mage takes my hands in his and closes his eyes. I follow suit because there's just something about him at tells me everything is going to be okay. I'm not sure what to expect when I feel a gentle hum start to radiate through my body. Something is happening.

CHAPTER EIGHT

DOMINIC

"Nothing a quick memory wipe can't fix though. He should get here soon. I'm just killing time with the human." As the words leave my mouth a sick feeling settles in my gut. Is that what I really want? To pretend like Vanessa never happened?

"You're such an idiot sometimes," the words ring through the phone. "Tell me about Vanessa." I don't hazard to question how Tabby knows my inner turmoil. It's Tabby. She's known me better than I've known myself since we were hatchlings.

I run a hand through my hair and sit on the edge of the tub. "It started when I first got here..." I go into a brief summary of our fake engagement, dinner, the massages — glossing over the fucking sexy details, and the tournament.

Once I finish, Tabby lets out an exasperated laugh. "You sound happy. Never thought I would see the day Dom falls for a human. I must be rubbing off on you."

"I'm not—" But the thought dies on my lips. I've been grinning like a fool this whole time I'd been talking about Vanessa. What the hell has this woman done to me?

"That is what I thought," she says, matter of fact. "So go spend time with your girl, call off the mage—"

"I can't do that."

"I did not call the mage on Blythe and you do not need to either, Dominic."

She's right. "Fuck it, I'll call you back when I'm on my way home."

I pull the phone away from my ear as a "whoop whoop" echoes through the phone.

"Was that Blythe?"

"Do not worry about it," Tabby says through a fit of giggles. "Go get your woman."

She hangs up then.

Damn it, I need to stop lying to myself. I don't want Vanessa to forget me. I don't want this weekend to end. I don't know where she lives or if she's even looking for a relationship, but I can't just let her leave without at least telling her how I feel.

I swing open the bathroom door, ready to gather my gaming champion in my arms, but I'm greeted with empty air. I look around, thinking maybe Vanessa's playing around. But as I venture from the perfectly made-up bed to the empty tub with fresh bottles lining its rim, and then to the closet decorated with empty hangers, panic seizes my chest. Did she get cold feet about the memory wipe? I run out into the hallway and spot movement at the elevators. A bald head, mismatched clothes, a stooped back. He doesn't need to be showing his grey tentacles for me to know the mage is here. And he's following someone into an elevator.

"Wait!" I call running for them but the doors have already slid closed. I slam into their painted metal surface with a hard thud just as the lift makes it to the floor below this one.

I eye the emergency staircase at the end of the hall. That won't do. The mage has been around for a long time and is good at what he does. He could have Vanessa's mind wiped by the time they make it to the lobby.

I grit my teeth. Now that this is happening, I know for a fact I don't want it to.

I won't let it.

I brace myself and grip the edge of the elevator doors, forcing them apart with ease. My gift of heightened strength doesn't get used too often but I'm thankful for it now as I gaze down the dark shaft. The elevator is only a few floors below. I can make it.

Just as it stops at a new floor, I take hold of one of the cables controlling its motion and repel down it, fireman style. I land on the elevator roof and release the cables just in time for them to start their descent again.

I get down on one knee and bang my fist into the roof. "I order you to halt at once, mage. Now stand back, I'm coming in." This time I punch the elevator like I mean it, my fist moving through the roof as if it were just a cardboard box.

Vanessa lets out a yelp of surprise.

A few more punches and I drop through the jagged hole I've created, landing beside Vanessa and the mage. We stare at each other for a moment and the panic starts to creep in. Am I too late?

Then her face breaks into an incredulous grin and her eyes sparkle. "You didn't tell me cecaelia have super strength — that's totally not in the game. What else have you left out?"

I let out a breath I didn't realize I was holding and envelop my human in a big hug. I lift her off the ground and she wraps her legs around me.

The mage clears his throat and I turn on him, blocking Vanessa from his sight.

"Not even a 'Hi Dominic, nice to see you'? You think it's appropriate to sneak in and steal my — Vanesa." What was I about to say there? My girlfriend?

The mage pats my arm, unfazed by my anger. "It's good to see you, dear boy. It appears the land is treating you well enough. Your muscles have shrunk a touch. It's not that noticeable though. As for your accusation: dear Vanessa found me whilst I was making my way to your suite. As always I am simply following orders, Dominic. You had instructed me to eradicate certain memories from this lovely woman and that is what I was in the process of getting started." The whole time he's talking, his hands are folded serenely in front of him and he speaks with a gentle logic. It's hard to stay mad at the man.

I grunt and wrap an arm around Vanessa's shoulders. "You have new orders now. Your services are no longer required. Apologies for wasting your time."

Vanessa ducks out from under my arm and stands beside the mage like it's two against one.

"The weekend's over, Dominic. It's time to go back to real life. It's been fun, but I'm not looking to be your means to an end to 'kill time'."

"Killing time? Vanessa, you've made this weekend not only bearable but fucking amazing. There's no one else I would have rather droned on about table linens with despite how much of an asshole I was in the beginning. I can't promise to be a ray of fucking sunshine all the time but I promise you are the furthest thing from just a way to kill time."

Vanessa's forehead softens a little and I take that as a good sign, so I scoop her up so we're face to face. She wraps her legs around me in a comforting gesture that reminds me how I would nest in my tentacles to sleep as a hatchling.

"On the phone with Tabby, I was an idiot," I continue. "I wouldn't let myself believe that I could actually like someone beyond sex and I was wrong. I was so fucking unbelievably wrong Vanessa."

"You have the emotional range of a toaster but it sounds like between me and Tammy, we'll get you sorted out," she jokes. But her eyes have gone glassy and she presses her face into my shoulder. "I'm not crying, you're crying," she says, her voice muffled against my hoodie.

I squeeze her back. "Not that I want you to turn into Niagara Falls but how would you feel about being my date to the wedding next year?"

She pulls back suddenly, eyes wide. "Dominic, that's a year away. What, are we going to do long distance in the meantime? See other people?"

My eyes go dark at that last suggestion. "You're mine now," I growl. Then clear my throat with the amendment: "if you'll have me."

She nods, hesitant but still squeezing me tight.

"And long distance isn't going to work for me. Not that it's going to be a problem for us anyway. I saw your paperwork when you signed into the tournament earlier. As a fellow resident of Passions Bay, I'd like to formally ask you out to a fantastic local sushi place."

Vanessa looks to the ceiling of the elevator, throws both arms in the air and shouts, "Thank you, universe!" Then to me, "I would be honored to accompany you to the wedding next year and I would love to go out with you."

My brow furrows. "I'm sensing a but..."

"But," she cringes, "I refuse to get food poisoning from Franks Sushi Bar one more time."

The mage, still standing patiently at the edge of the elevator, gives a hacking cough and spits a fat one at the ground. "Do not speak of Franks in my presence," he mutters.

I chuckle and press my forehead to Vanessa's. "Sweetheart, trust me when I say this is one sushi place you've never been to before and I guarantee you won't get food poisoning."

Her eyes light up at the thought of exploring cecaelia culture in her hometown.

"Then yes, I accept your invitation," she says. Then she brings her lips to mine in a slow, deep kiss.

I jump, almost dropping Vanessa, when a chorus of whoops and cheers sound out. I'd been so caught up in the moment, in Vanessa, that I didn't notice the bachelorette squad holding the elevator doors open to watch us like the best reality television they've ever seen. The tallest of the group, sporting a pink t-shirt dress and wearing glasses that resemble balls with a penis shooting up her forehead, holds out a hand to the mage who gives her a celebratory high five.

EPILOGUE: VANESSA

A briny ocean breeze tousles my curls and cools the couple hundred formally-dressed people gathered on the transformed beach for Tabitha and Blythe's ceremony. The sun hangs low in the sky as if waiting for the brides to kiss before it sets, while tealight candles twinkle up and down the beach. The brides in question positively beam at each other, standing under a driftwood arch draped in teal linens white hydrangeas. I don't know if they had some weather-controlling cecaelia on their side or if they just lucked out with this warm June day.

I toe off my wedges and press my feet into the warm sand under my chair, closing my eyes to enjoy the fresh air as the officiant does his best to describe love. That's the problem with words though — they're never enough to fully capture something as all-encompassing as love. It's something that can truly only be experienced.

I thought my lifetime of gaming, reading, and watching movies had given me a pretty fantastic idea of what being in a relationship was like. But the stuff my mind could conjure was nothing compared to the world Dominic opened up for me. I'm not just talking about experiencing cecaelia societies — nay, pods, or the mesmerizing glowworm coated cavern systems hidden right under the noses of all the humans in my hometown, though all that was insanely cool too. Dom showed me what it's like to have a best friend, broody cheerleader, and ten limbed fuck buddy all in one. No, that doesn't do him justice. Dom is that one person I don't ever want to live without. Not anymore.

I'm still living in my own rowhouse just across town from Blythe's mansion but Dom has been spending so much time with me that for all intents and purposes he's moved in. The man doesn't have many personal affects so aside from the single drawer full of clothes, the new home alarm system, new window locks, and the ringcam doorbell, my home is still very much me. We both like it that way. Obviously. I have pretty fantastic kawaii cybercore style.

I feel a tap on my leg and open my eyes.

Dominic is crouched beside me in his white button up, seafoam blue trousers and matching suspenders. This is the first time I'd seem him not decked out all in black and I have to say it does not suit him. While I appreciate Tabby and Blythe's colour scheme, the bright palette makes him look too cheery and that's just not Dom. It would be like trying to dress a panther in a pastel onesie — it's just not right.

"You're starting to lobster up," he whispers, pulling a travel size bottle of sunblock out of his pocket.

I examine my legs and then my arms. He's right. That telltale soft pink glow is starting to bloom on my pasty white skin.

With a smirk, he squeezes the bottle into his hands and starts lathering my skin. I would have argued that I can do it myself, but then I wouldn't get to feel his massive hands all over me.

Settle down, Vanessa, there's a wedding going on.

I look to the alter to see Tabby trying to fight back a smile in our direction. She's a total gem of a cecaelia and has been so supportive of Dom and I, bringing me into their world like I have every right to be here. Over her shoulder, her sister — Cecelia, the freaking ce-caelia queen — is shooting me daggers. I blow them a kiss and give a good-natured waggle of my fingers. Cecelia rolls her eyes. I don't take it personally. I've been forewarned that she doesn't particularly like anyone. I don't buy that though. I'm a firm believer there's someone out there for everyone. Probably a few someones, but all we need is one person to cheer her up.

When Dom finishes and I smell like a greasy coconut, he gives me a quick peck on the forehead, then resumes his place with the wedding party between Tabby and Cecelia. He is the finest maid of honor I've ever seen.

"Wanna dance?"

I twirl around in the middle of the dancefloor, my seafoam bubble dress spinning just a second after me, to see a red suited lumberjack of a cecaelia, hand extended to me.

Past the man's elbow, sitting at one of the tables with phone in hand, Dom is watching me with a glint in his eye. His thumb moves on his phone and a jolt of heat shoots through me from the vibrations in my panties.

My mind is momentarily scrambled. Something lumberjack man seems to be taking as a sign of his unfathomable sexual charm, if him puffing out his chest is any indication.

"I'm sorry, I must be overheating. I'm going to grab a drink," I say, trying to let the man down easy.

He starts to offer his help when suddenly Dominic is right behind him. His smug amusement is just barely contained behind that stoic exterior.

"I've got it, Sebastian. Thanks," he says with an heir of finality.

Lumberjack Sebastian looks between us, realization dawning on him. To his credit he's quick to retreat, muttering apologies to the both of us as he goes.

I smack Dom's arm. "You don't have to be so intimidating all the time. This is a happy occasion!" I gesture to everyone around us who suddenly erupt in cheers as the DJ starts up Taylor Swift.

Dom's hand moves in his pocket and I let out a sputtering cough to stifle the moan that almost escapes me as a pulse throbs beneath my dress.

Then Dom bends down to speak in my ear. "And you don't have to be deliciously ravishing but here you are."

I bite my lip, a flush creeping onto my cheeks.

It's getting late and the velvety deep blue night has crept into the sky outside. Everyone around us is blissfully drunk. Including the brides who are clumsily slow dancing to Taylor Swift's *Lover*.

"Okay, good game. You win. What now?"

With a squeeze of my hand, Dom leads me outside to the beach where the ceremony furnishings have already been put away. Instead of stopping in the sand he guides me into the warm ocean. Salty air brushes my hair out of my face.

"Any chance you're going to tell me where we're going?" I ask, loving the thrill of this.

Under the cover of water, Dom sprouts tentacles, gently wrapping me up in his embrace. "Nope, you're going to have to trust me, sweetheart. Deep breath now, okay?"

I nod. "Got it, cupcake." The moment air fills my lungs, Dom is off like an underwater jetboat, propelling us at insane speeds through the water.

I squeeze my eyes shut, focusing on the warmth of his chest and the tickle of water zipping past us. It's the same thrill I image my avatar would feel dropping into an arena. But this is real. This strong and not-so-secretly kind hearted cecaelia man who loves me and is whisking me away in the middle of the night is fucking real. Ten years ago, Vanessa the teenage hermit whose sole focus in life was trying to hide her gender from the other online gamers, could have never predicted this life for herself.

Not a minute later we emerge from the water and I gulp in fresh air.

I open my eyes to a sea of glowworms, coating this cavern in a soft blue glow.

"This is beautiful," I gasp. I'd seem the purple glowworm caverns of Dom's community, the Passion's Bay Cecaelia Pod. But the sight of these caverns were never going to get old for me. It's like something you'd find in a high budget fantastical RPG.

Dom pulls us out of the water and onto a big flat rock before loosening his grip of me. "It's an abandoned cecaelia cavern. I found it during my scout of the area before the wedding." A wicked grin crosses his face. "It's quite private in here. Which means we don't need this anymore," he says, reaching into my panties and plucking the remote vibrator from me.

I let out a whimper at the sudden emptiness left behind.

I hurry to rip off my cecaelia's clothes but he stops me, instead undressing me with painful slowness. It's so frustrating, though I quickly realize every time I protest, he stops and waits.

This tease.

With a couple of deep breaths, I'm able to shut up and let him finish undressing me. He tosses my dress to the other size of the cavern and peels off my nipple pasties, tossing them in the ocean.

I mock gasp. "I'm telling Tabby you're poisoning the ocean with silicone."

He's quick to cover my mouth with a tentacle. "You wouldn't dare," he counters. Though we both know he'll collect them on our way out.

I open my mouth and his tentacle slips inside, his suckers pulsing with that anticipatory adrenaline we're both feeling. I toy at his suction cups with my tongue carefully, and he shudders. Suddenly Dom scoops me up with four muscular blue tentacles and presses my back to his chest. His warmth is welcoming against the slight chill that's set in from the night air on my wet skin.

"How does it feel to have lost for the first time ever, Valkyrie Deathshroud?" he asks, using my Annihilation Royalle gamertag.

I shoot a glance at my cecaelia mate, excitement building in my throat. He's playing out a particular fantasy of mine and I'm here for it. Bring it on, Dom.

"I haven't lost, cupcake. I've got you right where I want you," I purr.

Tentacles grip my wrists and ankles in a show of dominance, then he leans into my ear. "You're adorable when you're helpless. I'm going to take my winnings now."

Still pressed firm against his chest so I can't anticipate his next move, a tentacle presses at my entrance. It finds no resistance on my part as it sinks up into me, the suction cups acting as the perfect ribbing that can't even be matched by any of my vibrators.

I moan and buck my hips, eager for more friction. Dominic doesn't move, a wicked grin on his face.

"I don't think so Valkyrie, you're at my mercy now. Which means I get to ravish you the way I please."

I jump at the unexpected sensation of a tentacle budding against my ass. No, not a tentacle.

His tentacle suddenly slips out of my wanting pussy to lather my juices against my anus. Then with a tender gentleness that totally doesn't befit an octo-person ruthlessly claiming me as their prize — not that I'm complaining — he pushes into me, little by little.

At first, I don't think there's any possible way for him to fit. But his patience pays off as he buries his tip in me. It's overwhelming as I stretch tight to accommodate his girth. The man's dick is like a literal eggplant, all thick and blue-purple. If the tentacles weren't convincing enough, you'd know he's not human from his intimidatingly impressive package.

"Are you okay"? he whispers in my ear.

Goosebumps prickle my skin at the tickle of his breathe.

"You can't best me that easily," I challenge.

A large hand suddenly grips my throat, pressing my head to his chest. "No more mister nice guy."

Fuck yes, I want to scream but my hand necklace makes it impossible.

His hips start rocking, the tip of his cock sliding in on out of my ass. The same rhythm is suddenly taken up by the tip of a tentacle worrying my clit and it's all too much. Dominic is everywhere, filling me up and holding me close. Knowing how much Dominic loves me makes the thrill of him ravishing me so completely in a cavern that much more sexy. I trust him completely. He can choke me, fuck me in the ass, and hold me captive in this little cavern and it's hot as hell because behind-the-scenes, I'm in charge. Dom would never do anything to hurt me or put me in any real danger. But the illusion of it? I can't get enough.

Dominic's hand tightens on my throat and my breaths come out in little pants as his hips and tentacle quicken place.

He comes with a full body-rocking force, ink filling my ass completely. That feeling is enough to tip me over the edge with him. Dom releases my throat and hugs me tight against him as we ride out of orgasms together.

Once we've caught our breaths, I get up off Dom's chest and look at my legs and the rock coated in black ink from Dom's release.

"We've made quite the mess," I tease.

Dom huffs. "Don't worry, we'll make a bigger mess next time."

I little seed of excitement plants itself in my stomach and I get up and head over to the cave wall, shooing away some glow worms.

"What in Poseidon's name are you doing?" he asks.

I don't answer as I dip coat my finger in Dom's ink and start writing on the wall. It's not exactly hieroglyphics, but the idea of immortalizing us here in this moment feels right.

I step back once I'm satisfied, so Dom can see too.

Winners:

Dominic of the Passions Bay Pod + Valkyrie Deathshroud

THE END

SEDUCING THE CECAELIA QUEEN

MAY MATTHEWS

Chapter One

CECELIA

"I just didn't think it would be as dull as a fucking barnacle on a rock," I lament. "I mean, look at her," I gesture to the massive stone statue of my late great grandmother, all mighty tentacles and swirls of water. A badass action shot if I'd ever seen one. The intricate heap of rock sits in the middle of our underwater courtyard, the beginning of coral starting to grow from its base, with the midafternoon sunlight dancing on the top of her stony head. "It looks like she was a busy Queen. Why can't I have that?"

"Darling I'm sure there's plenty to do," Mother says, brushing another cluster of algae off the statue's tentacle. "But you've barely been queen for a year. Just give it time."

I roll my eyes, snapping my fingers to summon over an eager-to-please cecaelia male whose been patiently waiting by the entrance to our community caverns in the cliffs. Then, readjusting myself on the cluster of squishy bubble coral, I guide his head to my center, between all my tentacles. I instantly relax the moment his tongue meets my sensitive flesh. It's not earth shatteringly orgasmic, but it brings me just the right amount of comfort to be able to tolerate my life in this moment.

I look to mother fussing over the statue. "What do you know, you're not Queen anymore. You're retired. Why are you still here? Go explore the world, join a cult, I don't care, but we don't need you here anymore."

Mother purses her lips. "Cecelia, my brash darling, I just got my grandmother back and I'm not going to leave her now."

You just got a statue back and that was a whole year ago, is what I don't say out loud. She's obsessed with the rock and there's nothing I can say to change that. I'm close to being all powerful as our cecaelia pod Queen, but my power with her ends there.

I wrap my tentacles around the male under me, forcing his tongue deeper into my heat.

"I don't know. Maybe I'll start capsizing ships like our ancestors did. At least that sounds like more fun than checking that our protective wards are up – which they always are, and keeping stock of our food supply – which has remained steady since I amended our trade deal with the upper coast pod.

Mother shakes her head.

"Relax you old fish, I'm joking." Kind of.

It's then the atmosphere changes. A shadow rolls over the statue and the current seems to shift. Mother and I look up in unison and see a long narrow profile with two appendages protruding the surface of the water.

"Get inside." I order, with a lazy flick of my wrist. I let the male out from my tentacle snare, his chin slick with my juices. He looks disappointed. Maybe I'll call him later. Mother dutifully follows after him and makes herself scarce.

Sending them away is just a precaution. We're not in direct danger. After all, we have a protective ward around this courtyard so if the human were to look down, all they'd see is the sandy ocean floor.

My concern is that a human is out this far at all. The cliff face next to us spans two miles south to the nearest human beach, which is the closest possible point in which someone can enter the water on a paddleboard. There doesn't seem to be a larger boat nearby either. I don't have a particularly good feeling about this.

But I'm bored and curious, so I angle myself behind the paddleboard and slowly swim closer, my tentacles propelling me with efficiency. I slow just as I make it to the surface and soundlessly poke my eyes out of the water. I'm met with the sight of a muscular, tanned back exposed through the low scoop-back of a skin-tight black one-piece bathing suit. Her arms and legs are covered in inked black designs and images. The woman removes her black ball cap, securing it beneath a bungee cord, revealing a sharp black pixie cut gleaming with sweat from the midsummer sun. It's hard to tell from behind, but she had to be in her late twenties at the most.

I hear the snap of a box clicking open, followed by the woman securing a snorkel mask to her face. As she fiddles with the head strap, I catch a glimpse of something that makes my heart sink. Snaking around her left forearm is a black and white tentacle tattoo.

I repress a frustrated sigh. Her tattoo and presence so close to my pod's cavern home is too much of a coincidence. It won't do to have this human snooping around here. If she swims down past the wards, she'll be able to see everything. Including the statue and our main cavern entrance. No, that won't do at all.

As the woman is readjusting the mask over her face, I slink back below the surface and let myself sink all the way to the ocean floor. The pillowy sand shifts under my weight as I crouch low on my tentacles. Then I give my muscles what they've been craving – a little action – as I launch myself upwards like a torpedo. With my arms braced to protect my head, I ram the center of the paddleboard.

The results are exquisite.

The woman topples backwards into the water, a tangle of limbs, and the board ricochets off the rocky cliff face.

My body is humming with that intoxicating shot of adrenaline.

I can understand my ancestors' fixation with sinking ships.

CHAPTER TWO

LEXI

The world spins in a tumultuous whirl of bubbles and sunlight, slick tendrils of flesh slithering past my body as I sink into Passions Bay.

If I were to believe the stories perpetuated by the small town locals and the gaming community alike, I'd have believed that I was about to die. But if the research conducted for my thesis is even remotely accurate, which I'm confident it is, I know better. I'm not in any real danger.

I close my eyes and still my body as I count to five in my head. When I open them again, the world has mostly steadied, save for a small trickle of water seeping into my mask from where my hair got stuck in the seal. But that small inconvenience is of no consequence because floating right in front of me, raven black hair fanned out around her sharp, angular face, deep purple tentacles undulating with the gentle current, is one of *them*. Top half of a human, bottom half of an octopus, just like so many myths have claimed.

"It's for the best," my oceanography professor's condescending words stuck with me all throughout my time as a classics student. "Kraken or cecaelia or whatever you call them really belong in the

study of mythology," he said. "I really don't see any zoological pro-
fessors supporting this topic down the line in academia."

Assuming my professor to be a wizened old man like Yoda or Mr.
Miyagi, I'd listened to his advice and swapped my Marine and Fresh-
water Biology degree for a Classics degree, which led me to do a Mas-
ters in Museum Studies and a PhD on the mythology of the cecaelia.
No, I've never had an interest in mythology or Latin or anything like
that. I just followed the disciplines that would allow me to further my
research on cecaelia. My colleagues all believed my research focused on
cecaelia as mythological creatures, but what I didn't tell anyone was
that this was real for me. Cecaelia were real and I was going to prove
it.

Despite different historical accounts conflating cecaelia with sirens
and harpies, I was confident they weren't an inherently malicious race.

The thumping of my heart in my ears was the result of my excitement, not fear.

I reached out a hand like I was approaching a stray dog.

The creature lunged at me. I couldn't see properly from my now
water-logged mask, but I could feel strong tentacles wrap around my
body, pinning my limbs to my torso. The creature had me clutched
tight against herself. Now my racing heart was caused by the panic
starting to set in. What if these creatures drowned me because they
thought I could breathe underwater? Or what if the creature crushed
me in her iron grip?

Suddenly I feel water rushing past us and I know we're on the move,
though I can't see anything through my flooded mask. She's taking
me somewhere. My lungs start to ache with the need for air and the
adrenaline coursing through my veins isn't helping.

You need to relax, I tell myself. *Slow your heartrate, conserve your breath.* With no other options available to me, I let my body go limp and close my eyes to preserve as much energy and air as possible.

What feels like minutes later, but is probably only a few seconds in reality, we break the surface of the water. I gulp in a glorious breath. The cecaelia releases me onto a rocky floor. Warm, humid air clings to my skin. I rip the mask off my face and blink the water droplets out of my eyes. I don't immediately understand where I am or what I'm seeing. The world looks purple.

A hand of long black manicured nails wraps around my upper arm and wrenches me to my feet.

I let out a yelp of surprise.

We're in a cavern, I realize, looking around, with walls coated in glowworms that bathe the space in a purple light.

"Are you injured?"

I turn to the owner of the steady voice. At five foot ten, I don't find myself looking up at people often. Now, however, I have to crank my head back to fully take in this creature before me. She stands tall, her torso of tanned flesh melding down into a fan of thick purple tentacles. The dozens of suckers on the underside of each tentacle seem to undulate like they're in an ocean current. It's hypnotizing. I look away from those eight limbs, realizing I'm staring. Then I see her full naked breasts which are framed by squared shoulders rolled back in a pose of absolute confidence I've never seen from any human.

She taps a tentacle under my chin. "Close your mouth human, you're not a guppy."

I'm aware I have no poker face, but can she really blame me?

"You're fucking real and you speak English!" I say far too loudly for this small echoey space. "You're literally right here. Standing in front of me. I knew it. I knew you were real!"

"Not too injured then, I suppose," she mutters, turning to drag me along with her.

A feeling beyond validation floods by system like a shot of ambrosia straight to my ego. I knew all along they were real. They *are* real. I'm not crazy; I'm right.

I let my hand brush along one of the creature's tentacles as it moves. It's surprisingly velvety and warm under my fingers.

"Don't do that," the creature says without breaking stride.

I open my mouth to ask one of the millions of questions racing through my mind, but the words evaporate on my lips when the creature drags me through a wooden door set into the stone.

All chatter in this new room comes to an abrupt halt as dozens of eyes fixate on me.

Still aglow in purple, this cavern chamber looks to have been converted into a redlight district sushi restaurant complete with ornamental chandeliers hanging amongst the stalactites, neon signs, and dining cecaelia. Tables and booths are scattered haphazardly around the small floorspace, but the room feels massive with its tall stony ceiling.

"What the hell is this place?" I mutter, failing to keep the awe from my voice.

"Your table is ready, my Queen," a tall, broad cecaelia male says. He looks like a tentacled bouncer dressed in a butler costume.

I shoot my abductress a wide-eyed look and, thinking quick, drop into a low bow. I'm not sure what the protocol is here but bowing is a pretty universal sign of respect. She's not just a mythological creature, but a freaking Queen!

A Queen who notably ignores me.

If this waiter is surprised that I'm dripping wet with two legs and a snorkel mask on my forehead, he shows no sign and just nudges me forward to follow after the Queen.

The other diners watch us head to our table in open curiosity and I watch right back. There are so many of them and they're beautiful. We pass by a sushi bar and a cecaelia woman behind a worktable assembling rolls with practiced efficiency.

"So sophisticated," I say.

The Queen brings us to a corner booth and I sit as directed, while she takes a seat across from me, draping her arms across the back of the plush red velvet seat, looking dangerous and sexy.

"Thank you, Petri," she purrs to the bouncer butler guy. "That will be all."

Petri bows and leaves.

Good. Even though she didn't acknowledge it, bowing was the right call from me. Now I'm all alone with this Queen. Is she actually radiating power or is that all in my head?

Two tentacles wrap around my ankles under the table and I can't help the pang of excitement that shoots through me. I glance at my tentacle tattoo wrapped around my wrist. The Queen takes notice too.

"Who are you?" she asks, voice soaked in suspicion.

"Lexi Pierce," I announce, reaching a hand across the table with a wide grin on my face. "And you are?"

She cocks her head like a seabird. "Why are you not afraid?" she asks, ignoring my question. Then she reaches out a tentacle to take a glass of wine from a passing waiter.

I pull my hand back, nonplussed. "I'll have a glass of wine too please," I call after the waiter. Then my stomach lets out a whale song as if to say, *what about me!* "On second thought, I'll have..." I look around for a menu.

The Queen snaps her fingers and a cecaelia male from a nearby table comes over and hands her his menu, bowing low, before scurrying away. She hands it to me.

I scan the laminated sheets listing dozens of colourful variations of maki, uramaki, sashimi, temaki, nigiri, tempura, and more. My mouth starts to water. This isn't even comparable to Frank's Sushi Bar back in town.

"You didn't answer my question, by the way," I point out. "You didn't tell me your name."

"That's correct," the Queen says. Then to the waiter, "We'll have an assorted platter."

The male bows low before leaving us.

Cecaelia are tricky creatures then. Noted. "But now I'm at a disadvantage. You know my name but I don't know yours," I keep my voice light so as not to come off as disrespectful. "I'm not answering any more questions until you contribute to this conversation." I really hope she doesn't call my bluff because I'm not someone who can just stop talking.

The Queen is silent but I can feel her eyes cataloguing every inch of me.

After ten whole seconds of suffocating silence, the waiter returns with a long silver platter. He places it on the table in front of us like we're royalty – *ahem she is*, I remind myself – and removes the lid. A smattering of textures and colours sits before me, the smell of fresh fish making my mouth water.

I immediately snag a reddish piece of nigiri and pop it into my mouth.

The Queen's lip quirks up, in a smug expression.

I freeze, dropping the remainer of the roll. *What, is it poisoned? No, why would she poison my food? Why wouldn't she?* "What?" Is what leaves my mouth.

"You humans are either stupid or reckless," she says. "You say your name is Lexi, though I suppose that is short for Alexa or Alexis?"

How did we pivot back to my name? "It's Alexis," I confirm. "Alexis Penelope Pierce." *Does this mean my food is safe?* I don't want to offend her, so I finish off the roll. It's fucking delectable.

Her smile widens, feral, and she leans forward onto her elbows, folding her talons together. "Like I said, stupid or reckless. Are you aware of what happened when Odysseus revealed his true name to Polyphemus?"

"Of course," I say, popping a dragon roll into my mouth. I've never had sushi this mouthwatering before. "It unleashed Poseidon's wrath on Odysseus."

She arches a brow and her grip around my calf tightens just a bit.

"Oh." The realization sinks in. I just gave a legendary sea monster my true name. My eyes dart around the space like something is going to come after me. "What's going to happen to me now?"

Again, she ignores my question. "It's nice to meet a human who knows her mythology. Tell me then, do you also remember what happened when Persephone ate a pomegranate seed in the underworld?"

My face heats up red like a stoplight and I burry it in my hands. How could I have been so stupid? I gave her my true name and ate her food. She probably just trapped me in this cave for eternity. Would that be so bad? What am I saying, I need sunlight! Ugh, so much for studying the classics when the minute I'm out in the real world, my disregard for those stories dooms me.

A sound pulls me from my thoughts. Cackling, deep and genuine.

I look up to see the Queen laughing, head thrown back, soft delicate neck exposed. Her voice echoes around the restaurant, but the other diners ignore us.

I awkwardly start laughing along. "Ya I can't believe how stupidly easy it was to trap me here too. Though while I'm here, I have a ton of questions for you." It won't do to dwell on mistakes, so I'm making the sanity-preserving choice to make the most of this.

She wipes a tear from her eye and releases her grip on my calves. "No, I just can't believe how gullible you are. Did you know that when you're thinking hard, it looks like the vein on your forehead is going to burst?" She snorts. "Human, I don't need a name or for you to eat my food to trap you here. Unless you've grown gills, you're stuck already."

A wave of relief washes through me. I'm not cursed or damned or otherwise magically trapped. I inadvertently wipe a hand over my forehead, trying to rub away the thinking-vein bulging there. *This is still the real world*, I remind myself. *Magic isn't real.*

"Do all of your kind enjoy playing pranks at the expense of others?" I ask, genuinely curious. Despite being a classics major, I still consider myself a biologist. I want to know everything about this species directly from the source. Is this a personality trait of the race or is it just her?

She shrugs her perfectly smooth shoulders, looking like a carefree goddess. "It's more fun this way." Then she winks.

My stomach does a cartwheel in response. I promptly stamp down that lust.

"So I'm just here for your entertainment? Interesting."

"Everyone is here for my entertainment," she says without missing a beat. "The reason you, in particular, are here is still a mystery. Care to enlighten me?"

Chapter Three

CECELIA

The human's entire being brightens at my question, completely ignoring the steel in my voice. She's a strange one. Every time I think I've pinned her, she bounces right back.

Now she looks like champagne bubbles ready to blow the cork. She slaps her palms on the table. "I'm so glad you asked! I don't mean to sound cocky, but I'm something of a cecaelia expert – or do you prefer kraken? Or maybe something in a language all your own? *Expert* is a bit of a misnomer because I really don't know all that much about your kind seeing as all my research has come from stories."

I let out a dramatic sigh. As repulsively adorable as her rambling is, my time is precious.

"Right," she says, taking the hint. "Anyway, I've spent my academic career researching your kind and my research had suggested Passions Bay would be a good place to look for you. So I took a chance and accepted the curator position at the Passions Bay History Museum so I could come out here and see for myself. And holy fucking shit you're actually here!" Her voice cracks at the end, her excitement getting the better of her and she clears her throat trying to regain her composure.

"I came here to learn more about your amazing race and maybe, with your permission of course, bring back something for my museum.

No. I realize I'm grinding my teeth at the thought of it. Of revealing our race to the humans. Not a chance.

Lexi seems to sense my thoughts and quickly adds, "Of course any artifacts would be framed as evidence of the *mythology* of cecaelia. I would never do anything to endanger your people – er cecaelia. People are too cruel to be trusted with this reality, what with our scientists and capitalism. Don't even get me started on billionaire pet projects. Do you go by cecaelia?

"Cecaelia is fine. You are here just to learn then?"

She finishes off the last roll on our platter which I'd barely touched. "And take a momento when I go if that's okay too," she adds.

I glance again at the tentacle tattoo inked around her wrist. Like a bracelet. Or a manacle. Slowly, an idea starts to form. It's as if the universe heard my laments of boredom and brought me Lexi.

"How would you like to make a deal?" I ask.

The entire restaurant freezes at my words, the clinking of cutlery and chattering all halting in sync.

Lexi starts to look around, so I quickly take her face between two tentacles and guide her gaze back to me before she can ask any questions. I don't want her impression of me tarnished by public perception yet.

"What kind of deal?" she asks, bringing a hand up to feel my appendage on her cheek. Her pupils dilate as she strokes.

A light tingle dances down my spine. I'd be lying if I said it didn't feel good.

I shake my head and bring my tentacles back to my sides.

"Petri!" I call.

My bodyguard returns in seconds.

"Parchment and quill please."

Lexi's eyes widen as both are placed in front of me, replacing our empty tray. "So archaic," she mumbles. "Don't you need ink too though?"

There's the money question. "I have ink. I'll need your help to get it though, little guppy."

Her mouth drops open, true to her new pet name. It closes and opens a few times, words seeming to fail her until finally: "How can I help?"

The scent of her lust reaches me, and I know I have her. I've been with male and female cecaelia before, alone and in groups. Orgies of tentacles and quickies in the throne room. It's all very common among our species. But the thought of being with a human for the first time is sparking a sense of excitement I thought I'd lost as far as sex goes.

I set the quill and parchment aside on the bench seat. Then I hop my ass onto the table, spinning around so that my tentacles are fanned out in front of Lexi.

Her face flushes a delightful shade of pink and she clears her throat again, "I need you to be as blunt as possible right now," she says, looking around at the other diners around the restaurant. Then she lowers her voice, "Do you mean for me to make you orgasm? Is that how I help get ink?"

"Is that a problem?" I ask, though her nipples peaked beneath her swimsuit already tell me the answer to that.

She quickly shakes her head, moving to kneel on the seat in one fluid motion. Then with an endearing hesitance, she brings her lips to mine.

I pull her flush against me with my tentacles and kiss her back with a rough fervor. She melts into me. Her mouth tastes of peppermint and it's so different from the salty taste of other cecaelia that I find myself wanting to taste all of her.

Yes, she is exactly the brand of excitement my life has been craving.

My tentacles gently slide over her warm body in all directions. Goosebumps prickle her skin at my touch. It feels so good to feel wanted like this and I have to admit that as much as I complain about humans, I'm looking forward to this.

I plunge my tongue into her mouth again, needing to be close to her, and feel her tentative hands roving their way down my stomach. She hesitates when she reaches the base of my tentacle.

"Here," I say. Cupping her hand in mine, I guide her around my tentacle to the space between all eight of my limbs. As soon as her fingers touch my core, I let out a small gasp.

I watch in part fascination and part pleasure as Lexi's hand explores my hot center.

"Fascinating," she breathes, "just like a human."

"No," I say, putting inches between our lips. "I'm not some specimen for you to study."

She looks up at me, then flushes as if just remembering that she's not in biology class. "Sorry."

I roll my eyes, "I want you to show me how sorry you are. I want to you show everyone here how sorry you are."

Her eyes dart away from me, scanning the room as if just remembering we're in public. The other cecaelia casually glance over between bites of their food.

"Get on the floor over there," I order, pointing to an empty space a few feet away.

She seems to make a decision then to not question me and cautiously kneels on the smooth stone floor.

"On your hands and knees," I add.

She does as instructed, though I can see her gulp.

"Good. Do you see the sign on the wall there?" I point to a framed needlepoint creation that reads, *The safe word is pelican.*

She lifts her head to look and scrunches her brow. "Pelican, got it. Do you do this here often?" she asks, genuinely curious.

"We are a sexual species," I say. "I would have expected a cecaelia expert to know that. Alas, I'll just have to show you, little guppy. You will call me your Queen and will slowly crawl to me."

She looks around once more at the other diners, closes her eyes, then takes a deep breath. When her eyes open again, the look she gives me is different from before, like she's turned off that part of her brain that keeps her questions flowing. Her eyes narrow suggestively and she drops her stomach, arching her back and starts to crawl. "I understand, my Queen." Her voice has gone husky.

Yes. "Now lose the suit," I say, testing her.

She stops, settling onto her knees and loops her thumbs through the straps. With a painful slowness that makes my stomach tighten, she starts to peel the fabric down her arms. It comes off her like a second skin, bearing the fresh fruit beneath. Before long, the material is bunched up in her fist and she's bared to the entire room. With short hair and no tentacles, there's no hiding anything. I don't think I've seen anyone quite like her before. Toned shoulders giving way to delicate pink breasts, pebbled in the air of this chamber. Her hips are decorated in a pattern of white stretch marks that snake down her thighs, turning into inked bolts of lightning. It's an artistic collage of ink and skin down both legs and arms. She's a living, breathing work of art.

"Crawl," I prompt her.

She smirks and follows my orders, inching closer, hands and knees to the smooth stony floor. Once within reach I whip out my tentacles and snag my prey, pulling her up on the table on top of me.

"I hope my little guppy is still hungry," I purr, pulling a nipple into my mouth and sucking hard.

She lets out a sharp gasp and I can feel her thighs clench around me. "Now treat me like the Queen I am," I say, freeing her breast.

"Abso-fucking-loutly, my Queen," she says, nipping at my breast on her way down.

She climbs down so she's standing at the edge of the table and yanks my body to the edge. Her confidence, her strength. Who is this human? Before I can ponder further, she's between my tentacles and her mouth is on me. The craziest thing happens: my mind goes blank. No thoughts of my boring duties or of my mother lingering in Passions Bay. It's all heat and throbbing, tongue, fulfillment, and pressure. So much pressure.

A torrent of pleasure erupts and my vision is a flash of white light.

I lay there for a moment catching my breath and then I remember her.

Lexi.

I sit up on the edge of the table to the most beautiful sight. Lexi on the floor on her knees, coated in the spray of my ink. Her mouth is agape, like she just got splashed by cold water.

A giggle, then an astonished laugh bubbles out of her and she looks at me, eyes sparkling. "Either I'm amazing, or cecaelia cum way more than humans."

I don't tell her it's the former.

Chapter Four

LEXI

"Mmm you look beautiful with my pleasure all over you, little guppy." Her voice is low and husky with postcoital satisfaction.

I give a blissful smile in return as I feel ink drip off my chin and trickle down my cleavage. Part of me can hardly believe I just ate out a stranger in a public place, but another part of me knows I'd do just about anything for this mythological creature I've dedicated years of my life to studying. Especially when they look like her.

I look around at a group of cecaelia males sipping on drinks, sparing me no more than cursory glances. Cecaelia are sexual creatures then. Here I was thinking that was just the human patriarchy's take on the myths. I'm more than happy I was wrong about that.

"Business time," the Queen announces, sliding back onto the bench seat, leaving a streak of ink behind.

I pull myself onto the seat across from her, not bothering to dress myself again. Contracting a business deal naked feels more right than doing so in a damp bathing suit. At least in these circumstances.

The Queen reaches across the table and dips her quill in the small ink pool that had gathered in the dip of my collarbone and starts to write in beautiful loopy calligraphy.

Beginning on June 30, 2024, Queen Cecelia of the Passions Bay Pod will loan Alexis Pierce, and by extension the Passions Bay History Museum, one different cecaelia artifact per week for the duration of this contract. Each artifact will be loaned for a period of one year.

In exchange, Alexis Pierce will swear fealty to Queen Cecelia, indefinitely.

For the duration of this contract, Queen Cecelia will protect and care for the physical and sexual needs of Alexis Pierce.

This contract will expire in four weeks time, on July 29, 2024.

She spins the page around for me to read when she's done.

I scan the parchment, heart skipping a beat when I get to the part about my sexual needs.

"Can I still return home to work?" I ask. "You know, so no one gets suspicious of my sudden disappearance?"

She gives a curt nod.

"I'm in," I say. I suddenly feel dizzy just thinking about all I can learn about this place and these creatures in a month's time.

The Queen hands me the quill and I sign on the dotted line just under her name.

Cecelia. Such a pretty name.

As soon as my quill lifts, the parchment shudders. I lean away just as it goes up in a poof of seafoam and gently disintegrates into thin air, leaving behind the scent of wood smoke.

"Holy shit, I'm going to need you to explain that one," I say, waving my hands through the empty space where the contract had just been.

She waves a hand. "Contract magic. That is a magically binding contract that neither of us can break. You belong to me now."

I want to ask more questions. I really do. But if I keep analyzing every little thing I'm learning today, I might actually go insane.
Whether magic actually exists or there's a scientific explanation is of
no matter. From here on out I'm just going to go with the flow. My
sanity will thank me later. I'll have time to think all this through after
the month is up and I'm back on land.

"Of course, contract magic," I say. "It'll be a pleasure to work with
you."

This time Queen Cecelia gives my hand a tight squeeze and a shake.
"It will be a very pleasurable experience," she replies.

The ink had hardened on my chin by the time Queen Cecelia brought
us to the bathing caverns. Cecaelia are such a clever species with
their intricate system of water tunnels connecting cavern chambers.
It makes it impossible for humans to enter or escape without a scuba
tank or a speedy cecaelia to guide you through the water. After being
carefully wrapped in Queen Cecelia's embrace, she shot off through a
series of underwater tunnels. I made sure my mask was on properly
this time so I could watch the journey. Admittedly I couldn't see
much; lots of darkness and creepy shadows cast from bioluminescent
coral smattered about. A dozen or so turns later we emerged in the
bathing chamber.

The room is made up of shallow pools of steaming hot water cast
in a soft light from blue glowworms and glowing coral that look like
something straight out of Atlantis.

"Mouth closed, guppy." Queen Cecelia drawls, pushing past me to slink into a pool the size of a hot tub.

I can't help it; cecaelia society is a marvel and I'm not going to just get over it after less than a day in its glory.

"I understand and all, but I will not stop gawking at how fucking amazing this place is," I say, following her into the pool. The second I lower my body into the steamy water, all the tension melts away. My shoulders fall, head lolling back on the rocky ledge. I sigh happily. "This is amazing. I don't know how you ever leave here."

"It gets old when it's your whole life," Queen Cecelia says, as she takes a bar of soap from the ledge and angles it at my face. "Humans don't spend their lives in onsens, do they now?"

She starts to scrub the bar on my chin and neck, lathering it up with her free hand. My senses are all lavender scented soap and the light scratch of long nails on my body. I'm not sure if it's the heat of the pools, the steam fogging up my brain, or my exhaustion from eating out monster royalty, but I let Queen Cecelia work on me in silence, the urge to fill it with my questions gone. I close my eyes and revel in the feel of her washing away the evidence of her pleasure, starting from my face all the way to my legs. When she gets to my thighs, I'm surprised to feel her fingers tracing the lines of my thunderbolt tattoos. I open my eyes to watch.

Slowly, she trails a nail across the jagged lines under water, taking care to follow the ink precisely. The tenderness she infuses into the act catches me by surprise.

"They don't have any meaning if that's what you were about to ask," I announce.

She startles as if she were in a trance. "I wasn't going to ask. Now turn around, you still have splatters on your back."

I do as instructed, smiling to myself as her soapy hands work a lather into my shoulders and back. Even though we're both still naked, the lust-filled tension from earlier is gone and has been replaced by a comfortable contentment.

I hear them before I see them. Four cecaelia women who look to be in their mid-thirties, enter from an adjacent chamber, chatting amongst themselves, laughing, scoffing. I know the moment they spot their Queen because they drop their voices and hurry into the furthest pool from us.

"You'd think you torture your citizens in your spare time for fun," I say in a low voice only Queen Cecelia can here."

Her hands pause on my back and I think she's going to respond except the silence stretches for a hair too long.

"You don't torture people though, right?" I ask, remembering I barely know this creature.

Her hands resume their circular scrubbing just below my shoulder blades. "It wouldn't hurt for others to think I do."

I try to turn to face her, but she holds me in place, facing away from her. "That's a really fucked up thing to do. By human standards anyway," I amend.

I feel her shrug. "Hatchlings can be brutal. Better to be feared than mocked, especially as Queen. I wouldn't expect a human nerd to understand."

I pull away from her hands and turn then, ready to defend myself when I spot the shit eating grin on her face. I settle for splashing her with the now murky grey water of our pool. "So being cruel is something unique to you, good to know. Maybe I'll just find another cecaelia to befriend. How would you like that?"

"That would be quite awkward seeing as our magical contract has bound you to be cared for by myself. Remember guppy, for the next month you belong to me."

Those words send goosebumps prickling down my legs despite the hot water. *I am hers.*

We soak in the pool in a happy silence. At one point my foot finds one of her tentacles and she doesn't stop me as I explore the ridges and bumps, suckers and flesh of her limb with my toes. If I'm not mistaken, she slowly pushes her tentacle closer to me for easier access.

In the silence though, I catch snippets of conversation from across the room. The four women.

"I don't have the time for my hatchlings... working late... males have all the freedom." The pieces start to take shape in my mind, forming a version of a story.

"Excuse me," I call, already vacating my pool to head towards the group.

They look to me, startled. It couldn't have been my lack of clothes that had them worried. Then I note their eyes glancing behind me to where I'm sure Queen Cecelia is scowling. But I push on. This is a chance to learn more about cecaelia society. "I couldn't help but overhear, are you having trouble with daycare?"

The women exchange a look. The petite one with blush tentacles and a snubbed nose speaks up. "Daycare?" She says it like it's a foreign word to her, which I realize now it probably is.

"You know," I say, squeezing into the pool between two of them, "having care for your children while you are working?"

"Yes!" the woman lights up, excited to be on common ground. "I work as an educator but my hatchlings are too young for schooling. I can't very well bring all twelve of them with me to work now can

I? And do you have any idea how expensive a nanny is for twelve hatchlings?"

The woman to her right rubs her friends back soothingly.

"Twelve!" I blurt out and quickly slap my hands over my mouth. "Wow I'm sorry, that was rude. Is it normal to have twelves chil-hatch-lings?" I ask.

The woman next too me with curly black hair looks me up and down and smirks. "Unlike humans, we can have up to six eggs at a time. But nobody chooses to get them all fertilized anymore. Partula here must have pissed off the wrong male because she had back to back full clusters of eggs fertilized."

"Without her consent," the woman to my left adds.

Suddenly a voice clears behind me. The whole pool seems to shrink at the Queen's presence. They immediately drop their heads. I do the opposite and turn to her, ready to share what I'd learned about her pod.

But when I look in her eyes, I see fire.

CHAPTER FIVE

LEXI

The second Queen Cecelia had stormed out, the room erupted in a cacophony of expletives. I sat, stunned not sure whether to go after the Queen or try and comfort these women. That is, until I remember that I can't follow her through the water tunnels on my own.

"A whole fucking week cleaning the kitchens – I don't have time for this!" the woman beside me wails.

"The vicious cunt," another spits. "Can't take the thought that her pod isn't perfect. Better to bury her head in the sand. Let me tell you, she's the most pathetic Queen we've ever had. Why couldn't her sister have taken up the throne? We'd be leagues better off."

"Woah, uncalled for," I say, flinching at the harsh words aimed at Cecelia. If I'd known that coming over here to listen in on some cecaelia community issues would send Cecelia into a rage, I never would have considered it. I don't want to upset her, but it looks like that's going to be a challenge seeing as I have no idea why this enraged her so much.

All four women shoot me a glare that would put Medusa's snakes to shame. "Are you a fucking masochist?" The one beside me snaps.

"You're seriously defending Her Cruel Majesty? Did you not just hear her punish us to a week of unpaid cleaning duty? The nerve of her."

I scooch back to sit at the edge of the pool and put a little distance between myself and the incredulous creatures before me.

"No, no, listen. I'll just talk to her. Clearly something triggered the Queen and once we get to the bottom of it, we can work through her emotions and have her see reason," I say.

They blink at me.

"Like adults." I add.

"Listen new girl," Partula says, running her fingers through her hair, "you don't know the Queen like we do. I'm sure she has some big emotions swirling in that inflated head of hers, but as optimistic as you are, you're not going to fix this. You can't change crazy after twenty five years."

I chew on the inside of my cheek, realizing I have something these women don't. I have hope in Cecelia. Everyone else has written her off as a vicious lost cause and maybe that's the problem. Does she even have anyone on her side or is it really just her against the world?

I stand abruptly, water dripping down my body. "Take me to her." I infuse my words with as much authority as I can muster.

In unison they all burst into a fit of laughter. Once Partula catches her breath, she shakes her head at me. "If one of us takes you, she'll punish us more. We can't take that risk, hun."

"Okay well maybe I can just walk to her," I say. I don't know where she is or how far I'd be able to walk without encountering a dead end or a water tunnel, but at this point it's worth a shot. And I'd be lying if the thought of exploring these caverns didn't excite me even a little.

I make for the wooden door the women entered from earlier, and step my bare foot onto a particularly smooth, slick rock. My foot shoots out from under me and I brace myself for impact, when something warm wraps around my arm. Partula is out of the pool and has a tentacle wrapped around my bicep.

"Thanks," I pant.

She steadies me up right. "The Queen would murder us if she knew you got yourself killed under our watch.

We had no real way of knowing where Cecelia had stormed off to, so Partula settled on bringing me to the Queen's chambers. As we approach the end of the water tunnel, Partula unravels her tentacles from around me, letting me swim the last few feet to Cecelia's room.

I nod my thanks and she salutes me in return, as if I'm a soldier about to sacrifice myself. I don't let the gesture get to me though because there's no turning back now. I brace myself for what I'm about to find. A room of broken furniture? For all I know of the cecaelia race, it could be a freaking sex dungeon.

I brace myself for anything and surface into Cecelia's chamber.

"Hello?" I call as I hoist myself onto the smooth stone floor.

For Queen's chambers, the space is relatively modest. The stone walls stretch into an impossibly tall ceiling dripping in stalagmites. Shallow canals of water line the perimeter of the room, full of cerulean and violet glowing coral that cast the room in cool light. The whole effect resembles an apocalyptic aqua chapel – if that were a thing. I might have been right about one thing though, I think, eying the padded manacles on the wall and floor. I can feel the blush wash over my face.

It isn't until the sound of water dripping from my body slows that a barely perceptible whimper reaches my ears. Curled up, facing away from me on a bed of giant bubble coral is the Queen of the Passions Bay Pod.

"Do you want to talk about it?" I ask, testing my weight on the squishy teal orbs that make up the coral bed. It shifts a little under me but is surprisingly comfy. I start to lean over Cecelia when she turns her head abruptly, startling me.

Instead of finding a broken, tear-streaked face, I'm met with that same fiery glare I'd seen in the bathing chambers.

I quickly stand, giving her space like she's an unpredictable hound. "I'm sorry, I thought I heard crying."

She looks down at her finger. "I got a paper cut, if you must know," she says. That's when I see the paper and quill in her other hand.

"You're writing a contract," I say.

"Are all humans as brilliant as you?" she jabs.

Then I spot the glass vial of ink on the side table next to her. "If you have ink, what did you need my help for?" I ask, realizing I already know the answer. "You didn't need my help, did you?"

"I don't *need* anyone's help," she says, turning her focus back to the contract she's half drafted. My eyes immediately fixate on "punishment" and "kitchens".

"You clearly do need my help," I say, snatching the parchment from her hands.

"You're out of line!" she snarls, spinning on me.

I hold out the paper and rip it clean down the middle. The parchment disappears in a sad imitation of the puff my contract went up in. *Maybe magic does exist after all.*

"You are not going to punish a group of women for complaining about their lives. That is so…" I think back to what Partula had said. "Barbaric," I finish.

She slowly gets to her tentacles, clearly enjoying the feeling of towering over me. "I keep them safe from humans, I bartered a trade agreement to ensure they're fed, and they have the nerve to repay me by complaining about their pathetic lives?" She lets out a low chuckle. "I will not let them or you walk all over me."

I shake my head, refusing to bow to her attempts at intimidation. I know she's not vicious to her core, just a little broken. Aren't we all?

"Do you have any friends?" I don't say it to be mean. It's a true question.

But Cecelia's anger hasn't simmered in the slightest. She moves so fast I barely log how she suddenly has me pinned against the wall, arms pinned above my head, her lithe body pressing into mine.

"I don't answer to you," she hisses.

That in and of itself is answer enough. This lonely Queen has nobody to turn to. Nobody to help her. Instead, she pushes people away out of a twisted sense of righteousness. She pushes people away yet craves their praise and love. It's a contradiction she's snared herself in.

Click.

My head snaps up to see my wrists bound in those wall manacles.

No. She's not this person. That fiery gleam in her eyes is a well-crafted mask and I'm not about to fall for it.

"You're their motherfucking Queen, so act like it." My voice echoes around the cavernous space and I'm proud of how authoritative I sound. "Your pod has complaints? Figure out how to make it better. Hell, ignoring them would be better than punishing them for legitimate worries. I know you ensure your pod has sustenance and physical protection from the outside world and that's a great start. But that's all it is. A start. Tell me, how do you spend your days?"

"Aren't we suddenly feisty," she says, voice dripping in condescension. "But if you must know I spend my days fucking and ensuring my pod is protected."

I flinch at her words. Best to rip off the bandage, I guess. It's good to know I'm just part of her daily routine. Nothing special.

"You are Zeus," I declare. "Protecting your people and fucking everything in sight.

She presses her body into mine as if to prove my point.

"The problem with gods," I continue, "is that alone, there is no balance. That is why the Greeks worshipped many gods. Gods and goddesses of the sea, of wine, of beauty, wisdom, war, etcetera, etcetera. In just resembling one god, you are lacking. You are forcing your people to worship only one god when they need more. Rightfully so. So instead of throwing a fucking tantrum and punishing everyone," I yank on my cuffs to prove my point, "you need to step up. And if there's something holding you back from your own potential, let me help you. You don't have to do this on your own. The good leaders never do."

When I'm done, Cecelia holds my gaze and I wish I could tell what she's thinking.

"Why did the complaints from those women *really* bother you so much?" I prompt, trying for a gentler approach.

Cecelia leans her forehead against mine and closes her eyes.

Chapter Six

CECELIA

I let out a resigned sigh. "My twin and I grew up different than the other kids and they didn't let us forget it." My voice is barely above a whisper. "I was bigger and stronger than my sister, so naturally it was up to me to protect us. We were heralded as loners because we didn't attend classes with the other kids. I hated our private tutors because of it. But when I got a little older and could actually comprehend the idea that we took special lessons precisely to hold power over the others one day as Queen, my whole mindset changed."

"I didn't know you had a twin sister," Lexi says with much more tenderness than I'd like. More than I deserve. "Why isn't she queen?"

"She chose to marry a human and pursue a life on land instead. Can't say I understand that choice in the slightest, but it left me the sole heir to the throne. So I'm not complaining."

Lexi lifts her face so that the tips of our noses are just touching.

"No, but others are." Her words are so delicate, I might actually make the mistake of believing she cared. "You are better than them. Once upon a time they chose to make you miserable. But you don't have to make that same pointless choice. You can make people's lives better and there is so much more power in that. Don't be Zeus. Be fucking Olympus.

As if Zeus himself were angry at that proclamation, a thrill like electricity shoots through my veins, hot and frenzied. I closed the inch of space between our lips and take Lexi's warm peppermint mouth in mine, pressing hard like I'll never get another chance. I drag my tentacles up her legs, tasting her skin with my suckers. Just as I'm about to reach her apex—

"Wait."

This human is going to be the end of me.

"In our contract, you promised to care for my physical needs, correct?"

"And your sexual ones," I point out.

"Unshackle me then please. I physically need to see you make things right with your pod before we do anything else."

I let out an exaggerated sigh and fetch the wrought iron key from my bedside table. "*Make things right*, you say. It's not that simple," I argue, unlocking the shackles.

Lexi's wrists break free, and she surprises me by enveloping me in a hug. I instantly melt into her embrace, feeling small in a good way for the first time in perhaps forever. I press my cheek to her breast and let her hold me for a long time.

I am Olympus.

I am Olympus.

I am Olympus.

The words have taken the shape of a mantra in my mind and they don't stop as I take the stage in front of my entire pod who have gathered to hear me speak. Their tentacles make them look like an undulating sea of velvet. My eyes stop when they find Lexi in her sleek black swimsuit, standing with Partula and her crew near the back of the cavern. Everyone but Lexi looks vaguely nervous and I suppose I only have myself to blame for that. Over this past year of my reign, I've practically trained them to fear me. Fear. Not respect. Lexi has opened my eyes to that distinction. If the universe really did send her to me, it wasn't just to alleviate my boredom.

Lexi shoots me a tacky thumbs up. She's a dork. But such a fucking sexy dork. After I fulfil my promise to her here, I'm going to enjoy slowly peeling that one piece off her body with my teeth.

I clear my throat in the middle of the stage, a raised stone platform at the center of this grand cavern chamber. "I've written a contract between myself as your Queen and you as my pod," I begin. I'm hardly aware of the words leaving my mouth because the whole time I'm focused on Lexi, who prompted me to outline this new contract to ensure I stick to my word of being a better Queen. Against my relentless advances, Lexi had us cooped up in my chambers for hours. Hours in which she wouldn't let me touch her where I wanted. Hours in which I actually started getting excited about this new contract we drafted for the pod. My cecaelia gift of contract magic will ensure that I stick to my word and focus more on the internal issues of our society and the individual grievances of my subjects. I used my knowledge of contracts to ensure I didn't write myself into a corner I wouldn't be able to deliver on while Lexi poured her heart and soul into ensuring empathy was at the heart of it. The result is a piece of magical parchment that will guide me towards fostering a thriving pod, not just a surviving one.

As I bring my speech to a close, the room fills with apprehensive chatter. Suddenly I'm not so sure about all this. They don't believe in me.

Then Lexi catches my attention again and she's beaming a brilliant white smile. My heart lurches in my chest and I remember what she told me before this assembly.

This is just the beginning. First you give them words, then a magical contract, then you will hit it home with inarguable action.

I take a deep breath. This is just step one. It's going to take time for them all to trust me and that's okay. That's reasonable even. You know what, I'm happy my pod has the collective braincells to not trust me right away. Effectively ruling over an intelligent lot is the *true* height of success after all.

"Alright everyone," I clap my hands together. "Please form a line at the front of the stage to sign this collective contract. I will remind you that under this contract you have no obligations. By signing you are agreeing to give me a chance to do better by you."

Lexi coughs hard into her fist.

"Oh yes and if you have any reservations about signing this contract, please schedule a meeting with me via Petri," I gesture to my bodyguard who looks stoic with a clipboard in hand.

Surprisingly nearly everyone, including Partula, line up to sign the contract. They're really willing to give me a chance after I'd treated them like garbage. Lexi comes up beside me, nudging my ribs with her elbow. "You did good Cece."

"Cece? Do you really think that is appropriate?" I ask, brow arched.

"Seeing as we're in business together and are contractually bound sexual partners, yes. Yes, I do." She bites the pillow of her lip and suddenly all the parts of her I want to bite come to the forefront of my brain. Something must show in my expression because she continues, her voice lowered "Want to get out of here?"

I snake my tentacle around her wrist, matching the tattoo she has there. "No". Her look of surprise with her mouth open just so is enough to completely undo me.

"Little guppy, what's wrong with right here?"

As if to wipe those words from my lips, she launches herself at me, wrapping her strong legs around my waist and pressing her mouth to mine.

We're still on the stage in a grand room teaming with cecaelia yet my mind is wholly fixated on this human koala'ed to my body.

I pull away and look Lexi in those olive doe eyes that are practically begging me for defilement. But I don't want to rush this. Lexi is like a bottle of wine during the prohibition. Something precious to be savored, and I want everyone to watch me drink tonight.

I peel Lexi off me with my tentacles and place her on her feet in front of me. She doesn't resist. Rather, she watches in rapt fascination, riding the wave of anticipation. I look her up and down, drinking in the sight of her. From her toned calves to the curve of her thighs, the red lines that are starting to form from where the hem of her swimsuit has started digging in from being worn too long. I see her tattoos in a new light now. The stretch marks morphing into lightning bolts striking a collage of images from grapes to books, fish to birds. She isn't just a single categorization. She isn't just a human. I am not just Zeus. We are more. Maybe together we can be everything.

"I want my whole pod to witness your beauty," I say, holding eye contact. "You are too spectacular to hide in my chambers."

She breaks into a cheshire grin and places her hands on her hips. "I want you to show me off."

I erase the distance between us and nip at the metal on her earlobe. "I want you to listen very carefully, little guppy. I am going to open you up like a gift and show you off to everyone in this room. I will touch you and tease you until this stage is slippery with your desire. And then, when you can't take it anymore, I will fill you up with my tentacles and make you scream. But nobody will hear you because you'll be too busy choking on my suction cups."

The peach fuzz on her neck stands on end at my filthy words.

I slowly drag my tongue over the shell of her ear. "Does that sound alright with you?"

"I would love for my sexy, mythological Queen to brag about me to everyone," she says, almost breathless. "I can't promise I can take all of you, but I sure as hell want to try. I remember the safe word."

Chapter Seven

LEXI

"Can I have your attention please," Cece's voice bounces off the walls of the cavern, instantly capturing the attention of the hundreds of cecaelia in the room. She stands tall and regal on her tentacles, shoulders squared, hands folded in front of her. "This contract you are all signing today was inspired by some wise words from this human right here. This is Alexis Pierce, Passions Bay History Museum Curator, my business partner, and my contractual plaything. I'm sure you can all sense her greatness from this contract. However I want you to *see* her greatness now."

All eyes turn towards me.

My heart is pounding like a jackhammer in my chest, equal parts nervous and excited. In my wildest dreams of finding the cecaelia race, this is a scenario I'd never imagined. At some point I must have stopped looking at this place, at Cece, as something to be studied. Without my conscious knowledge, that academic interest turned into something more to do with my heart than my brain.

She brushes a tentacle across the small of my back and then snakes it up my shoulder blade and over my shoulder. Then she expertly loops her limb under the strap of my swimsuit, tugging it down my arm.

She repeats the process on the other side with another tentacle, freeing my breasts from their fabric prison. With my swimsuit halfway off, she gently coils her tentacles around my upper arms and hoists me a few feet into the air. The audience of monsters watch, some with mild amusement, others with rapt interest, as Cece peels the black fabric the rest of the way off my body and lets it fall to the stage.

She raises herself up on her tentacles then to be level with me.

"Is my guppy comfortable?" She asks, lids heavy.

Surprisingly I am. The thrill of an audience does nothing to taper my excitement, for all my focus is on the cecaelia Queen in front of me, twirling the tips of her tentacles as if warming up.

"Yes, my Queen," I breathe.

"Perfect," she rasps and sucks one of my hardened nipples into her mouth.

When I audibly gasp at the instant pleasure, I can feel her smile against me. As her tongue and fingers toy with my nipples, I let go of any reservations I might have had left. I'm going to enjoy every second of this.

Soon enough, I feel Cece's mouth trailing lower, kissing my navel and lower until the point just above my heat. If she doesn't get on with it soon I'm going to lose my mind.

"Please, my Queen," I beg.

She mercifully obliges, but not in the way I expect. Stepping back and snapping her fingers, two cecaelia males join us on stage. I watch in a hazy fascination as their tentacles wrap around my arms and thighs, spreading me wide in the air like a Christmas tree topper.

Cece grins wide, taking me in.

I clear my throat and give her a look.

"Ugh okay. Claude, Maurice, thank you for your valuable assistance," she says to the males before returning her focus to me. "That's the last time you get to make demands. I'm in charge now."

"Yes, my Queen," I say, trying and failing to suppress a smile. I hadn't expected Cece to completely change her habits right off the bat, but this is a good start.

"We have a contract, Alexis, which states that you are mine for its duration. So I'm going to claim you here and now in front of my pod." She raises a tentacle and slowly drags it across my slit, her suckers torturing my sensitive skin.

I let out a moan of pleasure.

"For the duration of our contract, your pussy is mine," Cece says as she slips the tip of her tentacle into my heat. She slowly pumps in and out of me, gently at first. When I start to squirm she goes deeper, until her girth has me stretched as wide as I can surely go. Out and in, out and in, she sets a slow rhythm that has me humming.

"This is your first time being fucked by a tentacle, isn't it little guppy. Tell me, how do I compare to humans?"

She doesn't compare. Not in the slightest. I want to tell her it's like if a dragon dildo were to come to life in the form of a dangerously sexy Queen. But all my addled brain manages is a long, drawn out, "Fuck."

"Already that good? What if I were to take you from behind?" She slips out of me and the emptiness she leaves behind feels all wrong. Cece snaps her fingers and makes a hand gesture. The males seem to understand because they coordinate gripping me around the chest and hips and hold me sideways on my stomach in the air. Cece slips behind me and I lose sight of her.

"For the duration of our contract, your ass is mine," she declares and I can't help but squeal in surprise as she bites my ass cheek.

I playfully kick at her and she quickly restrains my legs in a couple of her many limbs. "Not fair, I only have two legs!" I call.

"I'll make it up to you," she says as she spreads my cheeks with her hands and presses her face into me.

I give a sharp intake of breath as the new sensation completely overwhelms me. She plays at me with her tongue, while her other tentacles start to explore, weaving through my hair, wrapping around my breasts, sliding through my folds."

I let out a strangled cry as she ever so slowly starts to press a tentacle into my ass and she pauses, completely misinterpreting my sounds.

"Please, keep going," I whimper. "You don't have to be so gentle, I've done this before. Well, not quite like this."

Her laugh is low and husky, just enough of a warning for me to brace myself. She pushes into me, filling me up from behind. She presses in so that I'm wrapped snug around her and then she abruptly pulls out.

"Such a beautiful flower," she says in a tone that would imply she's admiring a work of art in a museum.

"Fuck Cece, I'm going insane here," I call.

Suddenly she's right in front of me. "For the duration of our contract," she says again in a formal tone, "I own that demanding mouth of yours."

A tentacle creeps up my neck and over my chin, slipping inside my mouth.

Cece's signature salty taste fills my senses. This time though, she doesn't stop there. Her tentacles return to my pussy and ass and before I can register what's happening, I am filled to the brim with my Queen. As she starts a slow rhythm, all her limbs pumping me, she presses her lips to my forehead. The act is so sweet and so fucking hot I almost feel like crying.

"You're such a good girl" she whispers so that only I can hear.

My heart does a backflip in my chest and a tear actually slips out, equal parts courtesy of her rough fucking and gentle words.

She pulls her face back so I can see my surroundings again and that's when I realize the males have disappeared. It's just me and Cece. Cece everywhere.

"I let out an earth-shattering cry as I'm quickly pushed over the edge, a mass of shuttering flesh in Cece's arms.

A noise breaks through my exhausted panting.

Applause.

I look up from where I'm cradled in Cece's arms and tentacles on the floor of the stage.

Once the entire pod is done clapping, I look up at Cece. "At least they didn't ask for an encore. I don't think I can take any more. Not right now at least."

Cece snorts. "I told you in our contract that I'd take care of your needs and desires. And right now, you need to rest.

I turn over those words in my head, needs and desires. I have to ask her about what I'm thinking. "Does cecaelia society have marriages?" I ask. When her eyebrows shoot up, I quickly add, "Not that I want to get married or anything. It's just the wording of your contract vaguely resembles marriage vows."

"We have no need for marriage, we all care for each other," she says simply. "However I was at my sister's wedding last year and heard vows for the first time. I suppose you're not wrong.

We let those words hang in the air, both content to not put a label on whatever our relationship is.

CHAPTER EIGHT

EPILOGUE: CECELIA

You know that annoying feeling you get when you're in the shallows and the current keeps tickling you with a strand of seaweed but every time you think you've batted it away, there it is again? My family is like that. I try to ignore that seaweed feeling of my twin, Tabitha; her wife, Blythe; Tabby's bodyguard, Dominic; and his girlfriend, Vanessa; all watching me with ridiculous giddy expressions.

"If you keep looking at me like this, I swear I'm never leaving the ocean again," I call.

We're all gathered in the gallery of the Passions Bay History Museum for a pre-unveiling of Lexi's cecaelia display series. The actual unveiling will take place tomorrow with the public around but for now, it's an exclusive cecaelia plus one occasion.

I readjust my stance awkwardly on my legs. I don't often shift my form, much preferring the stability and resourcefulness of tentacles. But we all wanted to be safe in case anyone could spot us through the windows of this place.

My twin throws and arm around my shoulders. "Oh, do not be such a grouch, we are all just happy for you, big sister."

"Tabby, you're going to lose that arm if you don't remove it immediately."

She pulls her arm away, still beaming at me. "I never thought I would see the day you got a girlfriend."

"She's not my girlfriend," I argue.

Vanessa, who also happens to be Lexi's assistant at the museum, chimes in. "You know what we mean. Extended, extended, extended contract partner," she shrugs. "Is 'wife' more accurate then?"

I don't get a chance to deny her mildly accurate claim because Lexi appears from the back room looking excited in her high-waisted olive green trousers that match her round eyes and big shark tooth earrings dangling from her lobes.

"Thank you so much for being here everyone! I wanted you all to be the first to see our new display. Something I couldn't have put together without Cece." She winks my way.

Everyone claps and cheers as Lexi takes us around a corner to another section of the gallery. I let out a low whistle as I get my first glimpse of her work. I hadn't put much thought into it, but I was expecting something more along the lines of the artifacts I'd loaned her sitting in a glass case with tiny paragraphs of explanation beside each one. Not an indoor cave. That was really the only way to describe it. It looks like a room was erected inside of this gallery. The walls of it don't quite go up to the ceiling, like you'd see at temporary haunted house set-ups, except this one is painted to look like the wall of a cliff while a big red arrow on the floor directs people to enter through the doorway set into the wall.

"I want everyone to enter single file and enjoy the experience! Keep in mind, I did have to throw in some false information I'd gleamed from stories in order to throw off true cecaelia hunters.

Vanessa looks worried. "Are there actually cecaelia hunters out there?"

"There are people who dedicate their lives to finding bigfoot," Dom says, wrapping his arms around her from behind. "Do you think people would really draw the line at cecaelia?"

"Dom's right," Lexi continues. "I've met a few in my studies and I'd rather not direct them straight to your pod. All I'm saying is, don't feel the need to correct the facts in there. Enjoy!"

I stand back as Tabby and Blythe enter, followed by Dom and Vanessa. Their exclamations of surprise and delight when they're inside makes my heart swell with pride.

I saddle up next to Lexi, bumping her shoulder with mine. "Not too shabby, little guppy."

"Oh you haven't seen anything yet," she says, taking my hand and leading me into the faux cavern. Inside is a narrow maze made to look like a cavern system. Blue twinkle lights covering the walls wink at us as we pass, and the gentle soundtrack of water dripping reminds me of home.

I turn to Lexi who's the same height as me now that I've sprouted my legs. Her face cast in blue reminds me of that first day we met. "This is amazing, I hope you know that."

She beams, planting a soft kiss on my lips. "Trust me, putting all this together was much more fun than writing my thesis. And I figured this old museum could use a splash of something new to break of the monotony of all the old artwork from local estate sales." She tugs at the shark tooth dangling from her ear. "You know, I really couldn't have done this without you or your pod."

You'd think I'd be used to her sweet moments after three months together, but her earnestness still catches me off guard. "So you're happy I kidnapped you." I say wryly.

"I am happy you escorted me into a new world and held my hand through it all," she says carefully.

I snort. "What? Kidnapping isn't romantic enough for you?" I tease. When Vanessa had asked us how we met, Lexi had turned bright red at my account of the story. "Feel how you want about our meeting, it led you to me in the end. Moral of the story: kidnapping is always the right choice."

Lexi laughs, placing her hands on my back, shoving me ahead.

"Speaking of your pod," she says, "how have the new universal daycare laws been received?"

"Oh you know, imbeciles without hatchlings were skeptical and loud about their opposition at first, but once we put the laws in place it all seemed to work out. I'm pretty sure Partula's tentacles have turned a more vibrant pink since that weight was taken off her shoulders. Now I have a team looking into consensual egg fertilization."

Lexi hums her approval.

We pass glass cases mounted to the walls and hanging from the ceiling, each containing the artifacts I'd promised to her in our contract. Old coins, pearl jewelry, little stone statues of eels.

"You're going to love this next part," she says just as we turn a corner.

There they are. In a little glass protective box, mounted to the wall are the manacles I'd trapped Lexi in all those months ago when she'd managed to break down my walls and talk some sense into me.

I turn to her and am met with her lips on mine. Her kiss starts off innocent enough until I press my body into hers and she presses back.

"We never got to use those," I point out. "Please tell me you have the key."

Before she can reply, Vanessa pokes her head around the corner. "I just want to remind you that these are very cheap, flimsy walls, and we can hear everything. Do with that information what you will."

Then Dom's voice pierces the walls as he announces, "The technically not married, but totally married couple are about to go at it. Time to vacate the premises everyone.

Right on cue, Lexi's mouth drops open at his audacity. She's so predictable and so fucking perfect.

I tap her mouth closed with a finger. "Go get that key."

About the Author

May Matthews is a spicy paranormal romance author with a BA in English Language and Literature and an MA in Library and Information Science. She currently lives in Canada with her fiancé, two cats, and two huskies who love the winter way more than she does.

For more books by May Matthews, please visit her website at www.authormaymatthews.ca.

www.ingramcontent.com/pod-product-compliance
Lightning Source LLC
Chambersburg PA
CBHW070358200726
48294CB00003B/982